Dang...

R...

Carole...
London's ...
in her latest Harlequin® Historical miniseries.
But don't be fooled by their charm, because
beneath their lazy smiles they're deliciously sexy—
and highly dangerous!

Read all of the daring exploits
of these dangerous dukes in

MARCUS WILDING: DUKE OF PLEASURE
Available as a Harlequin Historical *Undone!* ebook

ZACHARY BLACK: DUKE OF DEBAUCHERY

DARIAN HUNTER: DUKE OF DESIRE

RUFUS DRAKE: DUKE OF WICKEDNESS
Available as a Harlequin Historical *Undone!* ebook

GRIFFIN STONE: DUKE OF DECADENCE

And don't miss

CHRISTIAN SEATON: DUKE OF DANGER

Coming soon

Carole Mortimer

Griffin Stone: Duke of Decadence

Carole Mortimer was born and lives in the UK. She is married to Peter and they have six sons. She has been writing for Harlequin® since 1978, and is the author of almost 200 books. She writes for both the Harlequin Historical and Presents lines. Carole is a *USA TODAY* bestselling author, and in 2012 she was recognized by Queen Elizabeth II for her "outstanding contribution to literature." Visit Carole at carolemortimer.co.uk or on Facebook.

Visit the Author Profile page at Harlequin.com for more titles.

Chapter One

July 1815, Lancashire, England.

'What the—?' Griffin Stone, the tenth Duke of Rotherham, pulled sharply on the reins of his perfectly matched greys as a ghostly white figure ran out of the darkness directly in front of his swiftly travelling phaeton.

Despite his concerted efforts to avoid a collision, the ethereal figure barely missed being stomped on by the high-stepping and deadly hooves, but was not so fortunate when it came to the back offside wheel of the carriage.

Griffin winced as he heard rather than saw that collision, all of his attention centred on bringing the greys to a stop before he was able to jump down from the carriage and run quickly round to the back of the vehicle.

There was only the almost full moon overhead for

gently stroke the long dark hair from over her face, revealing it as a deathly pale oval in the moonlight.

'Can you hear me?' His voice was gruff, no doubt from the scare he had received when she'd run out in front of his carriage.

Shrawley Woods was dense, and this rarely used track was barely navigable in full daylight; Griffin had only decided to press on in the darkness towards Stonehurst Park, just a mile away, because he had played in these woods constantly as a child and knew his way blindfolded.

There had been no reason, at eleven o'clock at night, for Griffin to take into account that there would be someone else in these woods. A poacher would certainly have known his way about in a way this barely clothed female obviously did not.

'Can you tell me where you are injured so that I can be sure not to hurt you again?' Griffin prompted, his frown darkening when he received no answer, and was forced to accept that she had once again slipped into unconsciousness.

Griffin made his next decision with the sharp precision for which he had been known in the army. It was late at night, full dark, no one had yet come crashing through the woods in pursuit of this woman, and, whoever she might be, she was obviously in need of urgent medical attention.

Consequently there was only one decision he could make, and that was to place her in the phaeton and

private war to be fought against the defeated emperor and his fanatical followers.

Just a week ago the Dangerous Dukes had helped foil an assassination plot to eliminate their own Prince Regent, along with the other leaders of the alliance. The plan being to ensure Napoleon's victorious return to Paris, while chaos ruled in those other countries.

A Frenchman, André Rousseau, since apprehended and killed by one of the Dangerous Dukes, had previously spent a year in England, secretly persuading men and women who worked in the households of England's politicians and peers to Napoleon's cause. Of which there were many; so many families in England had French relatives.

Many of the perpetrators of that plot had since been either killed or incarcerated, but there remained several who were unaccounted for. It was rumoured that those remaining followed the orders of an as yet unknown leader.

Griffin was on his way to the ducal estates he had not visited for some years, because the Dukes had received word that one of the traitors, Jacob Harker, who might know the identity of this mysterious leader, had been sighted in the vicinity.

It just so happened that three of the Dangerous Dukes had married in recent weeks, and a fourth wed just a week ago, on the very day Griffin had set out for his estate in Lancashire. With all of his friends

neath the covers of the bed in his best guest bed-chamber at Stonehurst Park, her abundance of long dark hair appearing even blacker against the white satin-and-lace pillows upon which her head lay, her face so incredibly pale.

'I assure you I do not mean you any harm,' he added firmly. He was well aware of the effect his five inches over six feet in height, and his broad and mus-cled body, had upon ladies as delicate as this one. 'I am sure you will feel better if you drink a little water.'

Griffin turned to the bedside table and poured some into a glass. He placed a hand gently beneath her nape to ease up her head and held the glass to her lips until she had drunk down several sips, aware as he did that those dark blue eyes remained fixed on his every move.

Tears now filled them as her head dropped back onto the pillows. 'I—' She gave a shake of her head, only to wince as even that slight movement obviously caused her pain. She ran her moistened tongue over her lips before speaking again. 'You are very kind.'

Griffin frowned darkly as he turned to place the glass back on the bedside table, hardening his heart against the sight of those tears until he knew more about the circumstances behind this young woman's flight through his woods. His years as an agent for the Crown had left him suspicious of almost everybody.

And women, as he knew only too well, were apt to use tears as their choice of weapon.

gown over her slender curves, revealing feet that were both dirty and lacerated beneath its bloodied ankle length. A result, he was sure, that she'd begun her flight shoeless.

There had also already been a sizeable lump and bruising already appearing upon her right temple, no doubt from her collision with his carriage.

But it was her other injuries, injuries that Griffin knew could not possibly have been caused by that collision, which had caused him to draw in a shocked and hissing breath.

The blood he had felt on his fingers earlier came from the raw chafing about both her wrists and ankles. She'd obviously been restrained by tight ropes for some time before her flight through his woods.

There were any number of explanations as to why she'd been restrained, of course, and not all of them were necessarily sinister.

Though he did not favour the practice himself, he was nevertheless aware that some men liked to secure a woman to the bed—as some women enjoyed being secured!—during love play.

There was also the possibility that this young woman was insane, and had been restrained for her own safety as well as that of others.

The final possibility, and perhaps the most likely, was that she had been restrained against her will.

Until such a time as Griffin established which explanation it was he'd decided that no one in his

changing into clean clothes and returning to spend the night in the chair at her bedside. He'd meant to be at her side when she woke.

If she woke.

She had given several groans of protest as Griffin had bathed the dirt from her wrists, ankles and feet, before applying a soothing salve and bandages, her feet very dirty and badly cut from running outdoors without shoes, and also in need of the application of the healing salve. Otherwise she had remained worryingly quiet and still for the rest of the night.

Griffin, on the other hand, had had plenty of time in which to consider his own actions.

Obviously he could not have left this young woman in the woods, least of all because he was responsible for having rendered her unconscious in the first place. But the uncertainty of who she was and the reasons for her imprisonment and escape meant the ramifications for keeping her here could be far-reaching.

Not that he gave a damn about that; Griffin answered only to the Crown and to God, and he doubted the former had any interest in her, and for the moment—and obviously for some days or weeks previously!—the second seemed to have deserted her.

Consequently Griffin now had the responsibility of her until she woke and was able to tell him the circumstances of her injuries.

Just a few minutes ago Griffin had seen her eyes

brought about only by generations of fine breeding, which held her mesmerised. He had a high intelligent brow with perfectly arched eyebrows over piercingly cold silver-grey eyes. His nose was long and aquiline between high cheekbones, and he'd sculptured unsmiling lips above an arrogantly determined jaw.

He was an intimidating and grimly intense gentleman, with a haughty aloofness that spoke of an innate, even arrogant, confidence. Whereas she...

Her lips felt suddenly numb, and the bedroom began to sway and dip in front of her eyes.

'You must stay awake!' The Duke rose sharply to his feet so that he could take a firm grip of her shoulders, his hold easing slightly only as she gave a low groan of pain. 'I apologise if I caused you discomfort.' He frowned darkly. 'But I really cannot allow you to fall asleep again until I am sure you are in your right mind. So far I have resisted calling the doctor but I fear that may have been unwise.'

'No!' she protested sharply. 'Do not call anyone! Please do not,' she protested brokenly, her fingers now clinging to the sleeves of his jacket as she looked up at him pleadingly.

Griffin frowned his displeasure, not in the least reassured by her responses so far. She seemed incapable of answering the simplest of questions and had now become almost hysterical at his having mentioned sending for the doctor. Had last night's bump

And in this instance, it could be being used as a way of not answering his questions at all!

But perhaps he was being unfair and she was just too frightened to answer him truthfully? Fearful of being returned to the place where she had been so cruelly treated?

It would be wrong of him to judge until he knew all the circumstances.

'Are you at least able to tell me why you were running through the Shrawley Woods in the dead of night wearing only your nightclothes?' he urged softly. He was not averse to using his height and size to intimidate a man, but knew only too well how easily those two things together could frighten a vulnerable woman.

'No!' Her eyes had widened in alarm, as if she had no previous knowledge of having run through the woods.

Griffin placed a gentle finger against one of her bandaged wrists. 'Or how you received these injuries?'

She looked blankly down at those bandages. 'I— No,' she repeated emotionally.

Griffin's frustration heightened as he rose restlessly to his feet before crossing the room to where the early morning sun shone brightly through the windows of the bedchamber, the curtains having remained undrawn the night before.

The room faced towards the back of the house, and outside he could see the stirrings of the morn-

His wife, although dead these past six years, had been such a woman. Even after weeks of courtship and their betrothal, and despite all Griffin's efforts to reassure her, his stature and size had continued to alarm Felicity. It had been a fear Griffin had been sure he could allay once they were married. He had been wrong.

'I am not—I do not—I am not being deliberately disobliging or difficult, sir,' she said pleadingly. 'The simple truth is that I cannot tell you my name because—because I do not know it!'

A scowl appeared between Griffin's eyes as he turned sharply round to look across at his unexpected guest, not sure that he had understood her correctly. 'You do not know your own name, or you do not have one?'

Well, of course she must have a name!

Surely everyone had a name?

'I have a name, I am sure, sir.' She spoke huskily. 'It is only—for the moment I am unable to recall it.'

And the shock of realising she did not know her own name, who she was, or how she had come to be here, or the reason for those bandages upon her wrists—indeed, anything that had happened to her before she woke up in this bed a few short minutes ago, to see this aloof and imposing stranger seated beside her—filled her with a cold and terrifying fear.

'What did you expect?' She struggled to sit up higher against the pillows, once again aware that she had aches and pains over all of her body, rather than just her bandaged wrists. Indeed, she felt as if she had been trampled by several horses and run over by a carriage.

What had Griffin expected? That was a difficult question for him to answer. He had completely ruled out the possibility that she'd sustained her injuries from mutual bed sport; they were too numerous for her ever to have enjoyed or found sexual stimulation from such treatment. Nor did he particularly wish to learn that his suspicions of insanity were true. And the possibility that this young lady might have been restrained against her will, possibly by her own family, was just as abhorrent to him.

But he had never considered for a moment that she would claim to have no memory of her own name, let alone be unable to tell him where or from whom she had received her injuries.

'You do not recall any of the events of last night?'

'What I was doing in the woods? How I came to be here?' She frowned. 'No.'

'The latter I can at least answer.' Griffin strode forcefully across the room until he once again stood at her bedside looking down at her. 'Unfortunately, when you ran so suddenly in front of my carriage, I was unable to avoid a collision. You sustained a bump upon your head and were rendered uncon-

'Perhaps,' he allowed coolly. 'But that does not explain what you were doing in the woods in your nightclothes.'

'Perhaps I was sleepwalking?'

'You were running, not walking,' Griffin countered dryly. 'And you were bare of foot.'

The smoothness of her brow once again creased into a frown. 'Would that explanation not fit in with my having been walking in my sleep?'

It would, certainly.

If she had not been running as if the devil were at her heels.

If it were not for those horrendous bruises on her body.

And if she did not bear those marks of restraint upon her wrists and ankles.

Bruises and marks of restraint that were going to make it difficult for Griffin to make enquiries about this young woman locally, without alerting the perpetrators of that abuse as to her whereabouts. Something Griffin was definitely reluctant to do until he knew more of the circumstances of her imprisonment and the reason for the abuse. Although there could surely be no excuse for the latter, whatever those circumstances?

He straightened to his fullness of height. 'Perhaps for now we should decide upon a name we may call you by until such time as your memory returns to you?'

descent? The hair flowing down her shoulders and over her breasts was certainly dark enough. But she did not speak English with any kind of accent that she could detect, and surely her skin was too pale for her to have originated from that sunny country?

And did the fact that the Duke had chosen that name for her mean that he thought her beautiful?

There was a blankness inside her head in answer to those first two questions, her queries seeming to slam up against a wall she could neither pass over nor through. As for the third question—

'I speak French, German and Italian, but that does not make me any of those things.' The Duke was obviously following her train of thought. 'Besides, your first instinct was to speak English.'

'You could be right, of course,' she demurred, all the while wondering whether he did in fact find her beautiful.

What would it be like to be the recipient of the admiration of such a magnificently handsome gentleman as Griffin Stone? Or his affections. His love…

Was it possible she had ever seen such a handsome gentleman as him before today? A gentleman who was so magnificently tall, with shoulders so wide, a chest so muscled, and those lean hips and long and elegant legs? A man whose bearing must command attention wherever he might be?

He was without a doubt a gentleman whom others would know to beware of. A powerful gentleman in

so many years of the deference shown to him by other gentlemen of the ton, and the prattling awe of the ladies.

Or the total abhorrence shown to him by his own wife.

He had been but five and twenty when he and Felicity had married. He'd already inherited the title of Duke from his father. Felicity had been seven years younger than himself, and the daughter of an earl. Blonde and petite, she had been as beautiful as an angel, and she had also possessed the other necessary attributes for becoming his duchess: youth, good breeding and refinement.

Felicity might have looked and behaved like an angel but their marriage had surely been made in hell itself.

And Griffin had been thinking of that marriage far too often these past twelve hours, possibly because the delicacy of Bella's appearance, despite their difference in colouring, was so similar to Felicity's. 'We have talked long enough for now, Bella,' he dismissed harshly. 'I will go downstairs now and organise some breakfast for you. You need to eat to regain your strength.'

'Oh, please don't leave! I am not sure I can be alone as yet.' She reached up quickly with both hands and clasped hold of his much larger one, her eyes shimmering a deep blue as she looked up at him in appeal.

dare to doubt, in any way. It was not only that he was so tall and powerfully built, but there was also a hard determination in those chilling grey eyes that spoke of his sincerity of purpose. If he said she would come to no harm while in his home and under his protection, then Bella had no doubt that she would not.

Her shoulders relaxed as she sank back against the pillows, her hand still resting trustingly in his. 'Thank you.'

Griffin stared down at her uncertainly. Either she was the best actress he had ever seen and she was now attempting to hoodwink him with innocence, or she truly did believe his assurances that he would see she came to no harm while under his protection.

His response to that trust was a totally inappropriate stirring of desire.

Was that so surprising, when he had seen her naked and she was such a beautiful and appealing young woman? Her eyes that dark and entrancing blue, her lips full and enticing, and the soft curve of her tiny breasts—breasts that would surely sit snugly in the palms of his hands?— just visible above the neckline of her—

What was he thinking?

Griffin hastily released her hand as he rose abruptly to his feet to step back and away from the bed. 'I will see that breakfast and a bath are brought up to you directly.' He did not look at her again before turning sharply on his heel and exiting the bed-

been able to do at such short notice, although he had instructed Mrs Harcourt to see about acquiring more suitable clothing for her as soon as was possible.

And if he was not mistaken, Bella had flinched the moment he'd spoken to her.

Unfortunately he knew that flinch too well; Felicity had also recoiled just so whenever he'd spoken to her, so much so that he'd eventually spoken to her as little as was possible between two people who were married to each other and often residing in the same house.

'My feet are still too sore for me to wear the boots provided,' Bella told him quietly, eyes downcast.

Griffin scowled slightly as he looked down at her stockinged feet. She gave all the appearance of a little girl playing dress up in those overly large clothes.

Or the waif and stray that she actually was.

He stood up impatiently from behind his desk. 'They will heal quickly enough,' he dismissed. 'I asked if you are feeling refreshed after your bath,' he questioned curtly, and then instantly cursed himself for that abruptness when Bella took a wary step back, her eyes wide blue pools of apprehension.

The fact that Griffin was accustomed to such a reaction did not make it any more pleasant for him to see it now surface in Bella. But perhaps it was to be expected, now that she was over her initial feelings of disorientation and shock in her surround-

gled and dull about her shoulders, and there was a livid bruise on her left temple, which the Duke said she had sustained when she and his carriage had collided the night before.

But those other bruises on her body were so unsightly. Ugly!

She had realised then how stupid she had been to think that he had chosen the name Bella for her because he had thought her beautiful!

Instead it must have been his idea of a jest, a cruel joke at her expense.

'No,' she finally answered stiffly.

Griffin had issued instructions to all of the household staff, through Pelham, that knowledge of the female guest currently residing on the estate was not to be shared outside the house, and that any attempt to do so would result in an instant dismissal. No doubt the servants would do enough gossiping and speculating amongst themselves in that regard, without the necessity to spread the news far and wide!

Griffin, of course, if he was to solve the mystery, had no choice but to also make discreet enquiries in the immediate area for knowledge of a possible missing young lady. And he would have to do this alongside his research into the whereabouts of Harker. But he would carry out both missions with the subtlety he had learnt while gathering information secretly for the Crown. A subtlety that would no doubt surprise many who did not know that the Duke of Rother-

not a rebuke.' He sighed his irritation, with both his own impatience and her reaction.

'Do not call me by that name!' Fire briefly lit up her eyes. 'Indeed, I believe it to have been exceedingly cruel of you to choose such a name for me!'

Griffin felt at a complete loss in the face of her upset. Three—no, it was now four—of his closest friends were either now married or about to be, and he liked their wives and betrothed well enough. But other than those four ladies the only time Griffin spent in a woman's company nowadays was usually in the bed of one of the mistresses of the demimonde, and then only for as long as it took to satisfy his physical needs, and with women who did not find his completely proportioned body in the least alarming. Or did not choose to show they did.

His only other knowledge of women was that of his wife, Felicity, and *she* had informed him on more than one occasion that he had no sensitivity, no warmth or understanding in regard to women. Not like the man she had taken as her lover. Her darling Frank, as she had called the other man so affectionately.

Damn Felicity!

If not for Harker, then Griffin would not have chosen to come back here to Stonehurst Park at all. To the place where he and Felicity had spent the first months of their married life together. He had certainly avoided the place for most of the last six

already gaping neckline to reveal her discoloured shoulders. 'And this!'

'Enough! No more, Bella,' Griffin protested as she would have lifted the hem of her gown, hopefully only to show him her abraded calves, but he could not be sure; an overabundance of modesty did not appear to be one of her attributes!

'Bella.' He strode slowly towards her, as if he were approaching a skittish horse rather than a beautiful young woman. 'Bella,' he repeated huskily as he placed a hand gently beneath her chin and raised her face so that he could look directly into her eyes. 'Those bruises are only skin deep. They will all fade with time. And they could never hide the beauty beneath.'

Bella blinked. 'Do you truly mean that or are you just being kind?'

'I believe we have already established that I am cruel rather than kind.'

'I thought—I did not know what to think.' She now looked regretful regarding her previous outburst.

Griffin arched that aristocratic brow. 'I am not a man who is known for his kindness. But neither am I a deceptive one,' he added emphatically.

She gave a shake of her head. 'When I undressed for my bath and saw my reflection in the mirror I could only think that, by giving me such a beautiful

And perhaps he had not thought of it because he had not wished for her to be a married woman?

But he knew better than most the embarrassment of a cuckolded husband, and Griffin's physical response to Bella was not something he wished, or ever wanted to feel for a woman who was the wife of another man. Not even one who could have treated her so harshly.

Indeed, marriage could be the very worst outcome to Griffin's enquiries regarding Bella; unless otherwise stated in a marriage settlement, English law still allowed that a woman's person, and her property, came under her husband's control upon their marriage. And, if it transpired that Bella was a married woman, then Griffin would be prevented by law from doing anything to protect her from her husband's cruelty, despite his earlier promise to her.

His arms tightened about her. 'Let us hope that does not prove to be the case.'

Bella had sought only comfort when she snuggled into the Duke's arms, seeking an anchor in a world that seemed to her both stormy and precarious.

Since then she had become aware of things other than comfort.

The way Griffin's back felt so firmly muscled and yet so warm beneath her fingers.

The way he smelled: a lemon and sandalwood cologne along with a male earthy fragrance she was sure belonged only to him.

taking her as his wife. Unbeknown to him, Felicity's father, an earl, had been in serious financial difficulties, and a duke could hardly allow his father-in-law to be carried off to debtors' prison!

Bella felt utterly bewildered by Griffin's sudden rejection of her.

Had she done something wrong to cause him to react in this way?

Been too clinging? Too needy of his comfort?

If she was guilty of those things then surely it had been for good reason?

She felt totally lost in a world that she did not recognise and that did not appear to recognise her. Could she be blamed for feeling that Griffin Stone, the aloof and arrogant Duke of Rotherham, was her only stability in her present state of turmoil?

Blame or otherwise, Bella now discovered that she had resources of pride that this austere Duke's dismissal, the ugliness of her gown, or her otherwise bedraggled and bruised appearance, had not succeeded in diminishing.

Her chin rose. 'I believe I do like books, Your Grace.' Stiltedly she answered his earlier question. 'Perhaps I might borrow one from this library and find somewhere quiet so that I might sit and read it?'

Griffin was feeling a little ashamed of the abruptness of his behaviour now. The more so because he had seen Bella's brief expression of bewilderment at his harsh treatment of her.

Griffin's mouth firmed as he brought an abrupt halt to the unsuitability of his thoughts. He could not *keep* Bella, even if she were foolish enough to want to stay with him. She was not a dog or a horse, and a duke did not *keep* a young woman, unless she was his mistress, and Bella was far too young and beautiful to be interested in such a relationship with a gentleman so much older than herself.

Nor did Griffin have any interest in taking a mistress. A few hours of enjoyment here and there with the ladies of the demi-monde was one thing, the setting up of a mistress something else entirely.

Even if his physical response to Bella was undeniable.

if it transpired she was a thief, then he could not be sure she might not steal all the family silver before escaping into the night. And she might do so much more if she were more than a thief…

No, despite his haughty aloofness, his moments of harshness, and that air of proud and ducal disdain, Bella could not believe Griffin to be anything other than a kind man.

Besides which, she had not imagined the physical evidence of his desire for her a few minutes ago.

She looked at him shyly from beneath her lashes. 'Then I can only hope, whoever they might be, that they do not find me *too* quickly.'

Exactly what did she mean by *that*? Griffin wondered darkly.

He had come to Stonehurst Park for the sole purpose of finding Harker; the last thing he needed was the distraction of a mysterious woman he found far too physically disturbing for his own comfort!

A conclusion he was perhaps a little late in arriving at, when that young woman currently stood before him, barefoot, and a guest in his home…

The mysteries of her circumstances aside, Bella was something of an unusual young woman. The slight redness to her eyes was testament to the fact that she had been recently crying, which he was sure any woman would have done given her current situation. But most women would also have been having a fit of the vapours at the precariousness, the dan-

ing my memory, and so relieving you of my presence quite soon, after all.'

Griffin knew that he deserved her sharpness, after speaking to her so abruptly and dampening her enthusiasm so thoroughly just now. He had been exceedingly rude to her.

But what was he to do when he was so aware of every curve of her body, even in that ghastly gown? When she had felt so soft and yielding in his arms just minutes ago? When the clean womanly smell of her, after the strong perfume and painted ladies of the demi-monde, was stimulation enough? When just the sight of her stockinged feet peeping out from beneath her gown sent his desire for her soaring?

Why, just minutes ago he had been thinking of *keeping* her!

Damn it, he could not, he *would* not, allow himself to become in any way attached to this young woman, other than as a surrogate avuncular figure who offered her aid in her distress. Chances were Bella would be gone from here very soon, possibly even later today or tomorrow, if his enquiries today should prove fruitful.

He deliberately turned his attention to the papers on his desk. 'Do not go too far from the house,' he instructed distractedly. 'We have no idea as yet who is friend or foe.' He glanced up seconds later when Bella had made no effort to leave or acknowledge what he'd said.

tereness of his face. Laughter lines had appeared beside now warm grey eyes, two grooves indenting the rigidity of his cheeks, his sculptured lips curling back to reveal very white and even teeth.

He was, quite simply, the most devastatingly handsome gentleman she had ever seen!

Perhaps.

For how could she say that with any certainty, when she did not so much as know her own name?

She gave a shiver as the full weight of that realisation once again crashed down on her. What if she *should* turn out to be a thief, or something worse, and last night she had been fleeing from imprisonment for her crimes?

She did not *feel* like a criminal. Had not felt any desire earlier, as she'd made her way through this grand house to the Duke's study, to steal any of the valuables, the silver, or the paintings so in abundance in every room and hallway she passed by or through. Nor did she feel any inclination to cause anyone physical harm—except perhaps to crash the occasional vase over the Duke's head, when he became so annoyingly cold and dismissive.

Except there weren't any vases in this room, Bella realised as she looked curiously about the study. Nor had she seen any flowers in the cavernous hallway to brighten up the entrance to the house.

That was what she would do!

When she asked Pelham for a blanket to sit on

book out in the garden, and try to forget that I am such a bad-tempered bore.'

Griffin was far from a bad-tempered bore to her, Bella acknowledged wistfully. No, the Duke of Rotherham was more of an enigma to her than a bad-tempered bore. As he surely would be to most people.

So tall and immensely powerful of build, he occasionally demonstrated a gentleness to her that totally belied that physical impression of force and power. Only for him to then address or treat her with a curtness meant, she was sure, to once again place her at arm's length.

As if he was annoyed with himself, for having revealed even that amount of gentleness.

As if he were in fear of it.

Or of her?

Bella gave a snort at the ridiculousness of that suggestion as she glanced at him, and saw he was already engrossed in the papers on his desk. He did not even seem to notice her going as she took her book and left the study to walk despondently out into the garden.

No, the differences in their stature and social standing—whatever her own might be, though it surely could in no way match a duke's illustrious position in society?—must surely ensure that Bella posed absolutely no threat to Griffin. In any way.

In all probability, the Duke was merely annoyed

stayed in his home without the benefit of a chaperone or close relative.

Inviting *his* only close relative to come to Stonehurst Park and act as that chaperone was totally unacceptable to Griffin; he and his maternal grandmother were far too much alike in temperament to ever be able to live under the same roof together, even for a brief period of time.

Perhaps he should send word to Lord Aubrey Maystone in London? He worked at the Foreign Office, and was the man to whom Griffin reported directly in his ongoing work for the Crown.

The puzzle of Bella was not a subject for the Foreign Office, of course. Nor was it cause for concern regarding the Crown. But Maystone had many contacts and the means of garnering information that were not available to Griffin. Most especially so here in the wilds of Lancashire.

Except…

Maystone had been put in the position of shooting one of the conspirators himself the previous month, and after that he'd become even fiercer in regard to the capture of the remaining conspirators. If Griffin were to tell the older man about Bella, he could not guarantee that Maystone would not instruct that Bella must be brought to London immediately for questioning, for fear she too was involved in that assassination plot in some way.

He might never see Bella again—

Her heart immediately started to pound in her chest, and the palms of her hands felt damp. What on earth could have happened to cause such a reaction in him?

'Your Grace?' She looked up at him uncertainly as he reached her side.

'Who are you?'

The glowering Duke ignored her, his countenance becoming even more frightening as he instead looked at the young gardener with cold and frosty eyes.

'Sutton, Your Grace. Arthur Sutton.' The young man touched a respectful hand to his forelock, his face becoming flushed under the older man's cold stare.

'You may go, Sutton.' Griffin nodded an abrupt dismissal. 'And I would appreciate it if you would take yourself off to work elsewhere on the estate for the rest of the day,' he added harshly, causing the bewildered young man to turn away and quickly collect up his tools ready for departing.

Bella felt equally bewildered by the harshness of Griffin's tone and behaviour. It was almost as if he suspected her and the gardener of some wrongdoing, of some mischief, when all they had been doing was—

'Oh!' She gasped after glancing towards the house to see that the library window overlooked this garden, and realised *exactly* what Griffin had suspected her and the handsome gardener of doing.

but Bella had not been standing scandalously close to Sutton, nor had she been behaving in a flirtatious manner towards him. Admittedly she had been smiling as she chatted so easily with the younger man, but even that was not reason enough for Griffin to have made the assumption he had.

Could it be that he had been *jealous* of her easy conversation and laughter with the younger man?

Was it possible that he thought, because of the unusual circumstances of Bella being here with him at all, that her smiles and laughter belonged only to him?

That *she* now somehow belonged to him?

'Bella?'

She stiffened and ceased her crying, but made no effort to lift her head from the pillow into which it was currently buried as she lay face down on the bed.

She made no verbal acknowledgement of Griffin's presence in her bedchamber at all. Correction, *his* bedchamber. As all of this magnificent house, and the extensive estate surrounding it, also belonged to him.

And she, having absolutely no knowledge of her past or even her name, was currently totally beholden to him.

But that did not mean Griffin Stone had the right to treat her with such suspicion. That he could virtually accuse her of flirting with Arthur Sutton. Or worse…

tired of waiting for her response to his initial overture, now sat down on the side of the bed.

'Bella?'

Her body went rigid as he placed a hand lightly against her spine. 'We both know that is not my name.' Her voice was muffled as she spoke into the pillow.

'I thought we had agreed that it would do for now?' he cajoled huskily.

Until they discovered what her name really was, Bella easily picked up on his unspoken comment.

If they ever discovered what her name really was, she added inwardly.

Which was part of the reason she had been so upset when she'd returned to the house just now.

Oh, there was no doubting this aloof and arrogant Duke had behaved appallingly out in the garden just now; he had spoken with unwarranted terseness to Arthur Sutton, and had certainly been disrespectful to her. His implied accusations regarding the two of them had been insulting, to say the least.

Bella's previous treatment, as well as her present precarious situation, meant that her tears were all too ready to fall at the slightest provocation...

Griffin Stone's behaviour in the garden had not been slight, but extreme.

Bella slipped out from beneath his hand before rolling over to face him, hardening her heart as she saw the way he looked down at her in apology. She

There was still that last lingering doubt in Griffin's mind regarding her claim of amnesia. Added to, no doubt, by his having just observed her in conversation with one of his under-gardeners.

What if she had been passing information on to Arthur Sutton? If her arrival here in his home had been premeditated?

Shortly before the assassination plot against the Prince Regent had been foiled several of Maystone's agents had been compromised. Griffin had been one of them.

There was always the possibility that Bella had been deliberately planted in his home, of course. That she was here to gather information from him as to how deeply their circle had been penetrated.

And he was becoming as paranoid as Maystone!

Nor was it an explanation that made sense, when Griffin considered those marks of restraint upon Bella's wrists and ankles.

Alternatively perhaps she had been talking to Arthur Sutton in an effort to find some way in which she might leave Stonehurst Park without his knowledge.

And what if she had?

If Bella were to disappear as suddenly as she had arrived, then surely it would be a positive thing, as far as Griffin was concerned, rather than a negative one?

He would not have to give her a second thought

Bella frowned as she pushed herself up against the pillows; she felt at far too much of a disadvantage with Griffin looming over her in that way. 'Should you not offer me an apology before making demands for explanations?'

The Duke's jaw tightened. 'I apologised a few minutes ago. An apology you chose not to acknowledge.'

'Because it was far too ambiguous,' she told him impatiently. 'As it did not state what it was you were apologising for.'

The Duke closed his eyes briefly, as if just looking at her caused him exasperation. As no doubt it did. He had not asked to have her company foisted upon him, and whatever his own plans had been for this morning he had surely had to abandon them. Also because of her.

His eyes were an icy grey when he raised his lids to look at her. 'It was not my intention to upset you.'

Bella raised dark brows. 'Then what was your intention?'

Griffin wondered if counting to ten—a hundred!— might help in keeping him calm in the face of Bella's determination to demand an explanation from him. 'I was concerned that Sutton might have been bothering you.'

A frown appeared between her eyes. 'How could that be, when I was obviously the one who had walked over to where he was working, rather than him approaching me?'

down the length of his aristocratic nose at her. 'I do not permit vases of flowers in any of my homes.'

'Why on earth not?' She gave a puzzled shake of her head. 'Everyone likes flowers.'

'I do not,' he bit out succinctly, a nerve pulsing in his tightly clenched jaw.

He was currently at his most imposing, his most chilling, Bella acknowledged. She had no idea why the mention of a vase of flowers should have caused such a reaction in him. 'You are allergic, perhaps?'

His laugh was bitterly dismissive. 'Not in the least. I am merely assured that the beauty of flowers is completely wasted on a man such as me.'

'Assured by whom?' Bella frowned her deepening confusion.

His eyes glittered coldly. 'By my wife!'

His *wife*?

Griffin, the Duke of Rotherham, the man who had saved her from perishing alone and lost in the woods, the man she felt so drawn to, the same man who had physically reacted to her close proximity this morning, had a *wife*?

A nerve pulsed in his tightly clenched cheek. 'Obviously because she is not here.'

Bella felt totally bewildered by the coldness of his tone.

'Then where is she?'

His eyes were now glacial. 'She has been buried in the family crypt in the village churchyard these past six years.'

Oh, dear Lord!

Why had she continued to question and pry? Why could she not have just left the subject alone, when she could see that it was causing Griffin such terrible discomfort? The stiffness of his body, the tightness of his jaw, and the over-bright glitter of his eyes were all proof of that.

But no, because she was irritated with him over his earlier behaviour, those ridiculous assumptions he had made concerning her conversation with Arthur Sutton, she had continued to push and to pry into something that was surely none of her business. Into a subject that obviously caused this proud and haughty man immense pain.

'Do you have children, too?'

His mouth tightened. 'No.'

'How did she die?' Bella knew she really should not ask any more questions, but the look on Griffin's face indicated that if she did not ask them now she might never be given another opportunity. And she wanted to *know*.

'No!' Griffin's hands moved up to hold those slender arms about his waist. 'Stay exactly where you are,' he ordered as his body relaxed against Bella's warmth and the soft press of her breasts against his back.

It had been so long since any woman had voluntarily offered him the comfort of her arms other than for that brief prelude occasionally offered before the sexual act began.

Griffin's eyes closed as he now savoured the sensation of just being held. Of having no expectations asked of him, other than to stand here and accept those slender arms about his waist. At the same time as Bella's softness continued to warm him through his clothing.

Griffin had not realised until now just how much he had missed having a woman's undemanding and tenderness of feeling. He had not allowed himself to feel hunger for those things that he knew could never be his.

He had to marvel at Bella, giving that tenderness and warmth so freely, when circumstances surely dictated she was the one in need of that comfort.

For the moment Griffin did not want to think about those circumstances, to give thought to the fact he knew nothing about this young woman. Why should he, when he had known even less about the women in whose bodies he had taken his pleasure

fever-bright, and the tips of her breasts had become swollen and sensitive beneath the material of her overlarge gown. She also felt an unfamiliar sensation low down between her thighs.

Griffin's large hands moved up to cup her cheeks as he tilted her face up to his, looking down searchingly. 'Are you a witch?' he murmured gruffly.

Bella could not look away from the compelling heat in those silver eyes. 'I do not think so.'

He gave a slow shake of his head. 'I think you must be.'

'Why must I?'

His eyes darkened, his expression grim. 'Because you have made me want you!'

Her heart leapt in her chest at the fierceness with which he delivered the admission.

There was such an unmistakeable underlying anger in Griffin's voice, telling her that he resented those feelings.

Because he still loved his dead wife, and the desire he now felt for Bella was a betrayal to those feelings?

Or was his anger with himself rather than her, for feeling that desire for someone he did not know or completely trust?

He gave a humourless laugh. 'You can have no idea how much I envy you, Bella!'

She blinked at the strangeness of the comment.

neath his, as he held back his hunger to plunder and claim but instead kissed her with restrained gentleness, her taste as sweet as the nectar between those petals. A nectar Griffin wanted to lap up greedily with his tongue.

Dear Lord!

Griffin groaned low in his throat, hungrily deepening the kiss as he felt the tentative sweep of Bella's tongue against his own like hot enveloping silk, her arms now clinging tightly about his waist as she pressed the soft length of her body eagerly against his much harder one. So eager, so trusting.

Damn it, he had made a promise to Bella to protect her while she remained in his household. And she had left him in no doubt that she now trusted him to ensure her safety. Even from himself.

It took every effort of willpower on his part, but he finally managed to gather the strength to wrench his mouth from hers, breathing heavily as he put her firmly away from him before releasing her.

He hardened his heart against the look of pained rejection in Bella's reproachful gaze. If he weakened, even for a moment, he would give in to the temptation to take her back into his arms. And he knew that this time he would be unable to stop kissing her, touching her, caressing her, and it would end with him craving more than she was ready to give.

'It is past time I returned to my study,' he barked before turning sharply to cross the room to the door.

just now, and she had revelled in the experience, in the rush of emotions she had felt at being held so tightly in Griffin's arms: pleasure, arousal, heat.

His rejection just minutes later had been as if a shower of cold water had been thrown over her.

She gathered herself up to her full height as she stepped away from the chair. 'I do not wish, thank you.'

Griffin gave a wince as he heard the hurt beneath Bella's haughtiness of tone.

Because he had called a halt to their kisses?

Because she had enjoyed them as much as he had?

But what other choice did he have but to stop? She was a young woman staying as a guest in his household. A vulnerable young woman he had offered his protection to for as long as she had need of it. She said she trusted him.

Yet surely he had just violated that trust?

He would not be accused of violating her too!

Griffin gave a terse inclination of his head. 'Do as you please,' he dismissed coolly even as he wrenched open the door to the bedchamber and made good his escape.

Bella blinked back the tears of self-pity that now blurred her vision. She would not allow herself to cry again.

She refused to cry simply because Griffin so obviously regretted kissing her.

But what a kiss!

from home at present. The butler had informed him that Sir Walter, an avid member of the hunt, was currently in the next county looking to buy a promising grey, and his wife was away until the end of the week visiting friends.

Not that the latter was any great loss to Griffin; several inches taller than her rotund and jovial husband, Lady Francesca Latham was exactly the type of woman Griffin least admired. A blond-haired beauty, admittedly, but Lady Francesca also had a cold and sarcastic sense of humour, and spoke with a directness that Griffin found disconcerting, to say the least.

All of those visits had been a waste of his time and energy anyway, as he had not managed to ascertain any information from his conversations in regard to Bella, or Jacob Harker.

So the slowness of Griffin's pace on his journey back to Stonehurst Park was not due to any lingering enjoyment of his afternoon, but more out of a reluctance to see and be with Bella again.

He no longer trusted himself to be alone in her company.

The way he had responded to her earlier was unprecedented. He'd experienced a depth of arousal that had resulted in his continued discomfort for more than an hour after the two of them had parted. He had breathed a sigh of relief when she had asked to have

'We were just finished afternoon tea in the servants' dining room when we heard such a screaming and carry on.'

'Bella?' Griffin knew he was the one who was now less than composed. 'Did someone attack her? If someone has dared to harm her—'

'No, no, it is nothing like that, Your Grace. It seems that she must have fallen asleep some time after lunch, and had a nightmare. Mrs Harcourt is up in her bedchamber with her now, but Miss Bella is inconsolable, and we did not know what to do for the best.'

Griffin was no longer there for the older man to explain the situation to; he was already ascending the front steps two at a time in his rush to get to Bella's side, throwing his hat aside as he hurried across the hallway to ascend the wide staircase just as hurriedly, all the time berating himself for having left Bella.

He should not have left her alone after all that she had so obviously suffered.

Nor should he have parted from her so angrily earlier, when *he* was the one who had been at fault for kissing her.

He was an unfeeling brute, who did not deserve—

'Griffin!'

He had barely stepped inside the bedchamber, his heart having contracted the moment he took in the sight of Bella's tear-stained face, when she jumped

dark hair from her face. 'We have agreed it shall be for now.'

'No,' she sobbed emotionally. 'I meant that it really is not my name.' She raised her head and looked at him, eyes red, lashes damp, her cheeks flushed. 'I believe my—my real name is—I heard someone in my dream call me Beatrix.'

She had spent a miserable morning in her bedchamber, pacing up and down as she'd tried to decide what she should do for the best. What was best for Griffin, not herself.

He was so obviously a man who preferred his own company.

A singular gentleman, who did not care to involve himself in the lives of others.

A wealthy and eligible duke, who had not remarried after his duchess died six years ago.

And *she* was responsible for disturbing the constancy of his life.

What Bella *should* do now was leave here. Remove herself from his home. Before news of a woman's presence at Stonehurst Park became known, as it surely would be if she remained here for any length of time. The last thing she wanted was to blacken Griffin's name.

Except she still had nowhere else to go, nor the means to get anywhere.

The tears of frustration she had cried had not

mouth and her eyes, and she'd been dragged kicking from her bed before something had hit her on the side of the head and she'd known no more.

She had tried then to wake herself from the terror she'd felt, but she had not succeeded, that terror only increasing as instead the next image had been of waking to the painful jolting of a travelling carriage as she'd lain huddled and bound on the hard floor, unable to see, speak or move.

Even so, she'd known she was not alone in the carriage, had been able to smell an unwashed body and hear another person breathing, sometimes snoring, as they'd slept, but never speaking, except when the carriage had stopped and she had been dragged outside and told to relieve herself. She had refused at first, having had no idea where she was or who was watching her, but had roughly been warned she would be left in her own mess if she did not do as she was told.

The dream gave her no idea of time, of how long she had been in the carriage when it had finally stopped and she'd been dragged outside. There had been the sound of a door opening and closing, a degree of warmth, before she had been pushed to the floor and she'd felt ropes being twined about her wrists and ankles as she had been secured in place. The cloth about her mouth had been ripped away and she'd gagged as some stale bread had been pushed

ings still with her even though she was now fully awake; the shaking of her body beyond her control.

Pelham had burst through the bedchamber door first, quickly followed by the housekeeper, the two of them doing all that they could to soothe and calm her.

Except Bella could not be calmed or soothed. Not once she'd accepted that she had not been dreaming. That they were memories that had returned to her.

Along with the knowledge that her beloved parents were both dead.

So what did her captors want?

What did she overhear?

Who had she told?

Tell me, tell me, tell me!

She sat up suddenly, eyes wide as she turned to look at a grim-faced Griffin. 'Jacob,' she breathed harshly. 'The man who held me prisoner was called Jacob!'

within him. To the point where he was now wary of anyone who was not family or a close friend. This left him with a very small circle of people: his grandmother, the Dangerous Dukes and their wives, and Aubrey Maystone. And recent events had only added to his distrust and wariness.

However, was it possible that she was innocently involved in his own reason for being in Lancashire? 'Jacob?' he repeated softly. 'Could this man you refer to possibly be called Jacob Harker?'

She gave a pained frown. 'I never heard his last name, only his first, and I believe even that was by accident.'

'Can you describe him?' Griffin prompted gently. 'Did he have any distinguishing marks? A scar, perhaps? Or a mole?' Recalling that Harker had a mole on the left side of his neck.

She shuddered. 'I never saw him.'

Griffin frowned his puzzlement. 'I do not understand.'

'Usually there was a blindfold secured back and over my ears. On the day I heard his name they had been questioning me again, and had not covered my ears sufficiently, so that I could hear a muffled conversation, more like an argument, between the two of them outside of where I was kept prisoner.' She swallowed. 'The second jailer was angry, and remonstrating with the first, I think because they had once again failed to get the answers from me they wanted.

'Only in the dream,' she answered dully. 'And only that one instance, when I was dancing giddily with my mother.'

That was, Griffin now strongly suspected, because shock and fear were responsible for causing her amnesia. The memories were obviously returning to her, even if only subconsciously, but her imprisonment, the harshness of her treatment, meant it would probably take time for all of her memories from before her abduction to return to her completely.

He might have wished she could forget her imprisonment and torture too!

Griffin's attempts today, to see if Bea belonged to a family in the area, had come to naught.

On his way out this afternoon he had instructed Reynolds, his estate manager, to check on any of the empty cottages and woodcutters' sheds within the estate, in the hopes that he might find some sign of where Bea might have been held prisoner. Her flight through the woods the previous night surely meant that Bea could not have run far dressed as she was and without footwear.

Bea.

How strange that he had chosen a name for her not so far from her own.

Tears dampened her lashes as she pulled abruptly out of his arms before standing up. 'I do not know how or when my parents died, but it must have been recently I think, because in my dream I attended

not be too many couples in society who had both died at the same time, and recently, and with a daughter named Beatrix.

Being so far away from London himself, Griffin now knew he had no choice but to write to Aubrey Maystone and ask him to look into the matter for him.

'Bea, I hate having to ask you to dwell on this any further just now, but...'

'If I have the answer I will gladly give it,' Bea assured him sadly, the grief, the dark oppression of her dreams, obviously still weighing her down.

He nodded. 'The questions the man Jacob asked. What were they?'

'They were the same two questions, over and over again. How much did I overhear? Who had I told?' She frowned as she gave a shake of her head. 'I did not know the answers then, and I do not know them now.'

Griffin realised that someone obviously *believed* that she knew something they would rather she did not.

And it was in all possibility something to do with the reason why Jacob Harker had left Northamptonshire so suddenly several weeks ago, and travelled up to Lancashire.

Something of relevance to the foiled assassination plot of the Prince Regent just weeks ago?

Harker's possible involvement in Bea's abduction would seem to imply that was in all probability the case.

already so upset.' He looked grim. 'I am more interested in the questions that were asked of you, and what significance they— Damn it!' he muttered in frustration as there was a brief knock on the bedchamber door. 'We will talk of this again once we are alone again.'

'I really do not think I can discuss my actual imprisonment any more just now, Griffin.' Her voice broke emotionally. 'It is too—distressing.' She was slightly ashamed of this show of weakness on her part, but was unable, for the moment, to think any more of her imprisonment and what her dreams had already revealed.

Her worst fear now—a fear she dared not talk of out loud—was that she might also have been violated.

She did not remember it, did not feel in the least sore between her legs. But perhaps she would not have noticed that soreness amongst the other bruises, cuts and abrasions on her body?

Just the thought of that smelly and disgusting man laying so much as a finger on her—

The dreams, revelations, that she had already had, about her most recent life, before Griffin had found her in the woods last night, along with the things she had not yet remembered, made Bea's position here now seem even more precarious than it had been previously.

If that were possible.

She was an orphan. And one whom no one seemed

primary ducal estate, and Bea's dreams now indicated they would not discover who she was, or to what family she belonged, as quickly as he might have hoped. Bea could hardly continue to stay here without some further offer of explanation being made to his household staff as to the reason for her sudden presence in their employer's home.

But surely her late arrival last night with the Duke, wearing only her soiled nightgown, gave instant lie to the claim she was his goddaughter?

If Pelham or Mrs Harcourt found his choice of explanation in the least surprising, then they gave no indication of it. The butler placed the tray of tea things on the table in front of the window, and the housekeeper placed the box containing Bea's new gowns on the bed, both acknowledging their employer respectfully before departing the bedchamber.

'I am sorry I could not pre-warn you of my announcement, Bea.' He grimaced ruefully once they were alone together. 'As I am sure you can appreciate, following this afternoon's upset, some further explanation for your presence here now has to be given.'

As Bea also knew, without his having to say it, that Griffin was a man who disliked intensely having to explain himself to anyone.

As the powerful and wealthy Duke of Rotherham he no doubt rarely felt the need to do so!

bruised body, than she was with the kindly butler's sensibilities.

She kept her eyes downcast as she turned away to look at the laden tea tray, noting the two cups and saucers. 'Will you be joining me for tea?'

'I think not, thank you,' Griffin refused stiffly, accepting that Bea was unwilling to discuss this any further just now, and knowing it was past time he removed himself from her bedchamber.

Despite her earlier upset, and his claim now of being her godfather, it was still not acceptable that he spend so much time alone with her in her bedchamber.

Even if a part of him wished to do so.

Being reminded of the intimacy of bathing her the night before, of kissing her, and holding her in his arms, listening as she talked of the nightmares, Griffin felt the tenuous strands of an emotional bond being forged between the two of them.

And it would not do.

He was not truly Bea's godfather, but a healthy and virile man of two and thirty who was totally unrelated to her, and who had several times responded to her in a physical way that was definitely not in the least godfatherly!

They did not as yet know Bea's true circumstances or age, but Griffin now felt sure she came from a good family, and that he was at the very least ten years her senior.

Did Bea feel up to bathing and dressing in one of her new gowns before joining him for dinner?

It would certainly be a *normal* activity, in a world that now seemed even more alien to her than it had before. Besides which, her afternoon spent alone had resulted in those mind-numbing nightmares, and she wished to avoid the possibility of experiencing any more of those for as long as was possible.

'Dinner downstairs would be lovely, thank you,' she accepted equally coolly, fully intending to ask Pelham if she might have a bath before then. She felt unclean after the vividness of her dreams, as if some of that filth and squalor in which she had been kept prisoner still clung to her.

Griffin gave her a formal bow. 'Until eight o'clock, then.'

Bea kept her lashes lowered demurely as she gave a curtsy, and remained so until she heard the door quietly closing as Griffin left her bedchamber.

At which time she released a heavily sighing breath.

Her dreams had truly been nightmares.

Her fragmented memories, of her parents, her abduction and imprisonment, the frantic madness of her flight from her jailer, were even more so.

And there was still that lingering doubt that she might have been physically violated by her captors.

If so, was it possible she might have buried that particular horrific memory so deep inside her it might never show itself again?

to ascertain any and all information he could about a missing young lady named Beatrix.

It would take several days but Griffin had felt better in the knowledge he had at least done something positive in that regard.

His estate manager had also asked to see him earlier, as he believed one of the disused woodcutters' sheds in Shrawley Woods might have recently been inhabited. Griffin had immediately ridden out to look for himself.

It was situated about a mile from where Griffin had found Bea, and whoever had stayed in the barely furnished shed had attempted to cover their tracks. But it was impossible to hide the stench of unwashed bodies, or the presence of a bloodstained bucket in the corner of one of the downstairs rooms—the same bucket Bea had struck Jacob Harker about the head with?

Griffin believed it was and his rage had grown tenfold as he'd stood and looked about him. The shed consisted of just two rooms, the floors were of dirt, just a single broken chair and table in one of the rooms, and no other furniture. The roof overhead sagged, and no doubt leaked in several places too. Several dark rags had been draped over the single square cut out of one of the wooden walls. No doubt to prevent anyone from looking in. Or out.

There was nothing else there to show recent habitation, no ragged blankets, fresh food or water, but it

even the butler's quiet presence in the room to be an intrusion.

Griffin realised his mistake as soon as the older man left the room as the intimacy of earlier suddenly fell over the two of them like a cloak.

Bea knew a sudden discomfort at being alone with her dashing Duke. Well, he was not *her* Duke. Griffin was most certainly his own man. Self-contained, aloof, and demanding of respect. But he *was* her very handsome rescuer, and several times Bea had sensed an awareness between the two of them that was not avuncular. And earlier today he had kissed her.

'The soup is delicious,' she remarked to fill the sudden silence.

'My cook here is very good.' He smiled slightly, as if aware of her discomfort.

Because he felt it also? Bea would be very surprised if too much discomforted this confident gentleman.

'Thank you for my new gowns.' There had been three gowns in the box Mrs Harcourt had brought to her bedchamber earlier, two day dresses and one for the evening, the blue gown Bea was now wearing, along with undergarments, a shawl and slippers. 'I hope—I hope that once I am restored to—to being myself again, that I shall be in a position to repay you.'

'A few second-hand gowns altered by the local

Griffin looked at her searchingly. 'Something else is troubling you.' It was a statement, not a question. 'What is it, Bea?' he asked sharply. 'Have you re-membered something else?'

Tears glistened in her eyes as she looked at him. 'It is what I do not remember that now troubles me.'

'Such as?'

She gave an abrupt shake of her head, no longer meeting his gaze.

'I would rather not put it into words.'

Griffin frowned darkly. Bea had been physically beaten, emotionally tortured, what else could there possibly be to—? 'No, Bea!' he gasped harshly. 'Surely you do not think—? Do not believe—?'

'Why should I not think that?' Bea dropped her spoon noisily into her bowl as she gave up all pre-tence of eating. 'I was alone with these men, and at their complete mercy for goodness knows how long. Surely in those circumstances it would be foolhardy to assume that—that one did not—' She could not finish the sentence, could not put into words this last possible horror of her captivity.

Once it had been thought of, Bea had been unable to put the possibility of physical violation from her mind. She had tried to appear calm as she'd joined Griffin in the dining room. Had been determined not to speak of her worries with him.

But the what-ifs had continued to haunt her.

To plague her.

Chapter Six

Bea found it impossible to fall sleep. She was *afraid* to fall asleep. For fear that more of those dreams might come back to haunt her. For fear that she might learn more from those dreams than she was comfortable knowing…

So instead of sleeping, she threw back the dishevelled bedclothes and paced her bedchamber long after she had heard Griffin pass her door, no doubt on the way to his own bedchamber further down the hallway.

What must he now think of her?

Nothing she did not think of herself, Bea felt sure!

Of course, she was not to blame if she had been violated, but that would not make it any less true. Any less of a disgrace. Whether she had been forced or otherwise, it would not change the fact that Bea was no longer—

Bea raised her hands and pressed her palms

you pacing and muttering to yourself as I walked past your bedchamber, and guessed that you would find it difficult to sleep tonight. That you would perhaps have thoughts of running away?' He came to a halt just inches in front of her, hooded lids preventing Bea from seeing the expression. 'The things you remember suffering are bad enough on their own, Bea. Do not torture yourself further with thoughts of something that might not have happened.'

Tears stung her eyes as she gave a shake of her head. 'That is all well and good for you to say, Griffin, but you cannot possibly understand.'

'Bea, I was once held prisoner myself.'

'You were?' She blinked up at him uncertainly as he spoke quietly.

'I was captured by the French after the battle of Talavera,' he admitted grimly; it was not a time he normally chose to talk about. To anyone. And yet he knew that he had to. That it was his only way of assuring Bea that he knew a little of how she was feeling tonight. 'I do not pretend to understand the devils tormenting you, but I know what it is like to lose your freedom, to have suffered physical torture. To know of the scars it leaves on the soul.'

'How long were you held prisoner?'

He shrugged. 'A week or so, until I too escaped. What I am really saying, Bea, is that we all carry scars about with us we have acquired from life, whether they be physical or emotional.'

lier, about what else might have happened to her, disturbed him almost as much as it did her.

The thought of any man—*any man*—laying hands on Bea, let alone the animals who had kept her a prisoner in such filthy conditions, who had abused her both emotionally and physically, was enough to fill Griffin with a murderous rage.

His hands now closed into fists as he fought against that anger, knowing that it served no purpose right now; Bea needed his reassurance, not his rage.

The time for Griffin to let loose the full extent of his fury would come if—*when*—he caught up with Jacob Harker.

Because he would find him. And when he did the other man would suffer as he had made Bea suffer.

'Of course,' he now agreed briskly. 'What else are godfathers for?' he added lightly, and knowing he was deliberately using that tenuous claim in the hopes of amusing her, but also as a means of attempting to place their relationship on a platonic footing.

As a means of convincing himself that his feelings towards Bea were indeed platonic.

A husky laugh caught in Bea's throat as she straightened. 'I believe I shall like having you for my godfather.'

Griffin had never felt less like someone's godfather—Bea's godfather, in particular—than he did as he followed her inside her bedchamber and closed the door behind them.

tion; even if Griffin were to ever attend such frivolities, which she seriously doubted, then she did not believe he would have noticed her existence.

Just as she had absolutely no doubt that she most certainly *would* have noticed Griffin, whatever the circumstances of their meeting!

He had such presence, was so tall and handsome, it would be impossible for any woman not to notice, or to be attracted to the charismatic Duke of Rotherham.

And yet he had never remarried.

Because he had loved his wife so much the idea of marriage to another woman repulsed him?

That had to be the explanation, Bea accepted wistfully.

Oh, but it would have been so wonderful to meet Griffin under different circumstances. For him to have asked to dance with her at a ball. To have him accompany her into supper. To have him call or send flowers the following day.

Bea brought her thoughts up sharply as she realised that all of those things seemed perfectly natural to her. That perhaps they had happened in her previous life?

Oh, not with Griffin, more was the pity, but she was sure she had danced at balls, and been accompanied into suppers by handsome gentlemen, and that they had called or sent flowers the following day.

of his hair more tousled than ever as his head lay on the pillows beside her own, his harshly chiselled features appearing much softer in sleep.

Bea's fingers itched to trace those finely arched brows. The sharply etched cheeks and the length of his aristocratic nose. As for those chiselled lips...

They looked so much softer when Griffin's mouth was not set in the habitually grim and determined shape it bore when he was awake. Lips so soft and inviting, in fact, that Bea's temptation to taste them became too much for her, her lids fluttering closed as she began to move her face closer towards his.

'What are you doing?'

Bea froze with her own lips just inches away from Griffin's, guilty colouring warming her cheeks as she looked up at him; she had been so intent on kissing the softness of his lips, she had failed to notice that Griffin had raised his own lids and was now looking at her with stormy grey eyes.

Angry eyes?

She moistened her own parted lips before answering him. 'I was...merely taken aback at finding you here in bed beside me.' She turned the explanation into a challenge, having no intention of owning up to the yearning she had known to kiss him, to taste the soft temptation of his lips.

Lips that were once again set in that grim, uncompromising line as he sat up in the bed before swinging his legs to the floor and standing up.

'Michael,' Griffin confirmed abruptly. 'You called out for him in your sleep.'

'I did?' Her expression remained uncomprehending.

He nodded. 'You kept repeating his name, and then you said, "Michael must be so alone, so very alone!" and then you began to cry.'

Griffin could still remember the clenching of his gut as Bea had called out for the other man in her sleep, and how she had shed tears because she could not be with him.

He had no memory of having fallen asleep on the bed beside her after he had sought to comfort her, but he did recall the weight of her obvious love for the other man as weighing heavily on his chest.

Because he had enjoyed kissing her?

Because he wanted to kiss her again?

Because he was growing fond of Bea himself?

Griffin briskly dismissed such thoughts as nonsense. He merely felt responsible for Bea, and was concerned as to what had happened to her and why. Saddened for her, too, because she seemed to be so alone in the world.

Except she obviously was not as alone as he had thought she was. Because she was obviously concerned for—loved?—a man named Michael.

Did this Michael love her in return?

Of course he did; how could any man not fall in love with Bea if she chose to give her love to him?

It would certainly be a first in this house for Griffin to be found in any lady's bedchamber in the morning, he acknowledged grimly. Even in the early days of their marriage Felicity had rarely allowed him entry to her bedchamber, and when she did she had always insisted that he leave again immediately after one of their less than satisfactory couplings, with the claim that she could not possibly fall asleep with his bulk in the bed beside her.

As Bea had done so easily and comfortably the night before.

And making comparisons of the way in which the two women regarded him was not only unproductive but also painful. It was like comparing night and day, rain or shine, when Bea was so obviously daylight and sunshine, after the dark and stormy years of being Felicity's barely tolerated husband.

His mouth tightened at those memories. 'I really do have to go now.' For the sake of his sanity, if nothing else! 'We will talk of this further over breakfast, if you wish.' He gave a terse bow before collecting up his boots and departing the room.

Bea was left momentarily stunned at the abruptness with which Griffin had left her. She felt guilty as she realised how her presence here was a constant inconvenience to him. Firstly, by his being forced into the position of becoming her saviour at all. And latterly, her presence here, an unaccompanied and

how the afternoon sun made her hair appear a particularly beautiful shade of blue-black against the pale lemon of her gown.

These past three days had been surprisingly companionable ones, with just the two of them sitting here together in the library during the day, he working on estate business, Bea quietly engrossed in her book, before they dined together in the evenings. Their conversations together had flowed surprisingly easily, Bea proving to be an intelligent woman, knowledgeable and able to discuss many subjects, despite her continued lack of memories of her own former life.

Much as Griffin had once imagined he would spend tranquil days and quiet evenings at home with his wife. Except Felicity had never wanted to sit companionably with him anywhere. In fact, towards the end of their marriage, it had become almost too much to expect her to even occupy the same house as him.

He frowned as he once again firmly put thoughts of Felicity from his mind to turn and look at his butler standing in the doorway. 'Show Sir Walter into the blue salon, if you please, Pelham,' he instructed impatiently.

'Very good, Your Grace.' The butler bowed out of the room, closing the door quietly behind him.

'Sir Walter Latham?' Bea repeated curiously as she closed her book.

'A neighbour who was away from home when I

somewhere, and Griffin was no doubt respecting her own silence on the subject.

Consequently they had fallen into an easy routine during the past three days. Bea, in keeping with her decision not to be any more of a burden to Griffin than necessary, had chosen to suffer her sleepless nights in silence. Although she often fell asleep here in the library beside the fire during the daylight hours, reassured, no doubt, by Griffin's presence across the room.

'I am perfectly content to remain in here until after your visitor has gone,' she now assured him lightly.

'This should not take long.' He deftly straightened the cuffs of his white shirt beneath his jacket, looking every inch the Duke in his perfectly tailored dark grey superfine, black waistcoat, pale grey pantaloons and highly polished black Hessians. 'Amiable he might be, but one can only listen to so much of Sir Walter's conversation on the hunt and the magnificent horse flesh in his stable!' he added dryly.

Bea chuckled softly. 'He sounds a dear.'

Griffin considered the idea. 'He is most certainly one of the more congenial of my closest neighbours.'

'And is there also a Lady Latham?'

'She is something less than a dear,' Griffin assured him with feeling, more than a little relieved that Lady Francesca appeared not to have returned

ish to do so, when at any moment her memories might come back to her, and she would then be returned to her former life, her time spent at Stonehurst Park, and with Griffin himself, both things she would rather put to the farthest reaches of her mind.

Griffin had ensured there had been no opportunity for a repeat of the kiss they had shared that first day, but that did not mean he did not feel desire every time he so much as looked at her.

A desire that Bea, so innocently trusting, obviously did not see or recognise.

Or return.

'I won't be long,' Griffin said harshly before turning sharply on his heel and leaving the room, instructing Pelham regarding Bea's tea, and striding determinedly into the blue salon to join Sir Walter.

At the same time as he determined he must put all thoughts of kissing Bea again from his mind.

Or try to, at least.

'Oh, my, yes.' The older man grinned as he resumed his seat opposite. 'I managed to buy myself a beautiful grey hunter.' He nodded his satisfaction.

Griffin nodded. 'Your butler informed me that Lady Francesca is away from home at the moment?'

'She was in London for part of the Season, acting as chaperone to my young niece. The two of them are presently making their way to Lancashire via several house parties.' The older man grimaced. 'I cannot abide London, or house parties, but for some reason Francesca enjoys all that social nonsense.'

Griffin smiled in sympathy; he too hated all that social nonsense, but had been forced to attend a certain amount of those functions when he was Felicity's husband. 'I am sure you will be pleased to have her and your niece returned to you.'

'Without a doubt,' Sir Walter agreed jovially. 'A house needs a woman's presence in it to feel anything like a home— Ah, but I apologise, Rotherham.' He frowned his consternation. 'That was in particularly bad taste, even for me.'

'Not at all,' Griffin dismissed dryly, having become accustomed to Sir Walter's bluntness over the years.

Besides which, Felicity's presence in any of his ducal homes had always made them feel less like a home to Griffin, and towards the end of their marriage that had been reason enough for him to wish

Bea's precise age, although he did not believe she could be any older than twenty.

The older man's eyes lit up with interest. 'Then no doubt Lady Francesca, once returned, will wish to invite you both over to dinner one evening while you are here, so that my niece and your goddaughter might become acquainted?'

'That will not be possible, I am afraid,' he refused smoothly. 'My goddaughter is still in mourning.'

'But surely a private dinner party is permissible?'

'I am afraid not. Bea's emotions are still too delicate at present for us to give or receive social invitations. Another time, perhaps,' he dismissed briskly as he stood up and rang for Pelham in conclusion of the conversation.

'Of course.' Sir Walter rose to his feet as he took the hint it was time for him to leave. 'It really is good to see you back at Stonehurst Park again, Rotherham,' he added sincerely.

'Thank you.' Griffin nodded.

'You must at least ride over and see my new hunter when you have the time.'

'Perhaps,' Griffin replied noncommittally.

'No doubt the young ladies in the area are also delighted at your return,' the older man added dryly.

Griffin did not dispute or agree with the statement as Pelham arrived to escort Sir Walter out, knowing it was his title the young ladies coveted. And he had learnt his lesson the hard way, in that regard!

swept up in a sophisticated cluster at her crown, with several loose wisps at her temples and nape.

She looked, in fact, every inch the beautiful and composed young lady of society that these past three days had convinced Griffin she truly must be.

A *unprotected* young lady of society, whom Griffin was finding it more and more difficult to resist taking in his arms and making love to!

'I do have other ducal responsibilities besides you, Bea,' he answered her with harsh dismissal. 'I cannot spend all of my time babysitting and mollycoddling you!'

'Of course.' It was impossible for Bea not to hear and inwardly flinch at the impatience in Griffin's tone. Or to feel hurt at being referred to as a responsibility. Even if that was what she so obviously meant to him.

It had been very silly of her to allow herself to grow so comfortable in Griffin's company these past few days. So comfortable, in fact, she had hoped that their time together might continue indefinitely.

Griffin was a duke, and, more importantly, he was a very handsome and eligible one. Her presence here, her unknown origins, must also be curtailing his own movements. Was it so surprising he did not wish to be burdened indefinitely with the responsibility of a young woman he did not even know, and, moreover, one who might very well turn out to be anything, from a thief to a murderess!

What was a man expected to do in such circumstances as these?

Bea was not his wife, nor was she related to him in any way, but for the moment she was his ward, and those tears glistening in her eyes indicated that, even if she was not crying, she was at the least very upset.

Should he follow Bea, and once again offer his apologies for his harshness? Or should he leave her to the solitude she was so obviously in need of?

He had respected Bea's need for solitude last time. Just as in the past Griffin had always respected Felicity's obvious aversion to his company, and his apologies for having offended her in some inexplicable way, by choosing not to intrude upon her solitude. But Bea was nothing like Felicity, and furthermore Griffin was well aware that it was he who was now responsible for her upset.

Bea was, without a doubt, a woman of great strength and fortitude, as she had demonstrated by her survival of her captivity and beatings, followed by her eventual escape. But even she must have her breaking points, and it appeared that Griffin's ill temper was one of them.

No doubt because he had become the only true stability in her world at present.

Griffin did not fool himself into thinking Bea felt any more for him than that. She was totally dependent upon him for everything, including the clothes she wore. At present, he was the only thing standing

possibly having caused him embarrassment when Pelham returned to the dining room and found her gone.

She drew in a deep steadying breath as she fortified herself for going downstairs and facing Griffin again.

Only to come to an abrupt halt the moment she opened the door to her bedchamber and found Griffin standing outside in the hallway, his hand raised as if in preparation for knocking.

She gave a nervous smile. 'I was just coming downstairs to speak with you.'

'As I am here to speak to you.'

Bea stepped back in order to open the door wider. 'Please, come inside.'

Griffin stepped reluctantly into the bedchamber, aware that it was probably not wise. He noted how at home Bea had become in just a few days; there were combs and perfumes on the dressing table, the gown she had worn that day was draped over the chair, with a pair of matching satin slippers left on the floor beside it.

He turned back to Bea as she stood nervously in the centre of the bedchamber. 'I feel I owe you an apology and explanation for my behaviour earlier,' he began.

'I wish to apologise for having been so unreasonable earlier—'

Bea broke off as she realised that they had both

And there is always the possibility that there will be no news at all, or that Maystone may be away from home when my letter arrives,' he added grimly.

Bea accepted there might be delays that might occur in the delivery of Griffin's letter. Even if his friend did receive the missive, there was no guarantee that he would be able to garner any information about her. If that should be the case, she had no idea what she was going to do next. She could not remain with Griffin; that would be expecting too much, even from a man as generous as he. In which case, she had a week at most in which to formulate plans for her own future.

'You are not to worry about this, Bea.' Griffin frowned as he saw her look of concentration. 'There is no rush for you to leave here. You eat no more than a mouse, and are almost as quiet as one!'

A mouse?

Was that truly how Griffin regarded her? As a *mouse*?

Bea might have no memories of flirtation or society, but even so she was sure that being described as *a mouse* was not in the least complimentary. Or that she behaved in any way like one.

Griffin realised from Bea's dismayed expression that he had somehow spoken out of turn again, when he had meant only to reassure. The dealings between men and women really were as volatile to him as a

him to take what was in front of him, and to hell with the consequences!

Would Bea accept or reject him if he were to take her in his arms and kiss her again?

Would she accept him out of gratitude, for all that he had done and was still doing for her?

Griffin did not want any woman to accept his kisses out of gratitude.

Bea frowned at Griffin's continued silence. She believed that before her abduction she must have been a tactile person, a woman who liked to touch and be touched in return.

Because at this moment she wished for nothing more than to reach out and touch Griffin, to feel his arms close about her, to be crushed against the hardness of his chest and thighs, to lose herself in his strength and power, to feel *wanted*.

Was she imagining the hunger she saw burning in the depths of eyes? Was it possible he felt the same need for touch, for warmth, that she now did?

His wife had died six years ago but Bea did not deceive herself into believing a man as handsome as Griffin would not have occupied many women's beds in the years since.

Dared she hope, dream, that he now wished to occupy *her* bed, and it was only his sense of honour that was holding him back from doing so?

She moistened her slightly parted lips with the tip of her tongue. 'Griffin...'

Could the warm feelings she now felt towards Griffin be so very wrong?

Her life was already in such turmoil, did she really want to add to that confusion by complicating things even further?

The answer to that question was *yes*!

It had become sheer torture for her to be so much in Griffin's company these past few days, and at the same time so aware of the barrier of formality he had erected between the two of them. To be aware of his deliberately avuncular attitude towards her.

A deliberation that had not been present in those glittering eyes just minutes ago when Griffin had looked at her so hungrily.

Were her own feelings, her emotions, sure enough at present for her to know exactly what she would be doing if she were to meet the fire she believed she had seen in his gaze?

A mouse, he had called her, when in truth the only reason for Bea's quiet these past few days had been in the hopes of making her presence here more tolerable for him, to make herself less visible, so that she appeared less of a burden to him.

Whatever her station in life might have been before her amnesia, Bea knew with absolute certainty that she could not possibly have been *a mouse*. Griffin had also called her a woman of fortitude, and Bea did not doubt she was a woman of determination and resolve. Anything less and she would not have sur-

Chapter Eight

So much for his claim that he needed to work,
Griffin acknowledged several hours later as he sat
sprawled in the chair behind the desk in the library,
a single lit candle on his desktop and the glow of
the fire in the hearth to alleviate the darkness of the
room behind him.

He had removed his jacket and cravat from earlier,
several buttons of his shirt he'd also unfastened for
added comfort, his thoughts ranging far and wide,
before inevitably coming back to the exact same subject.

Bea.

His fingers clenched on the arms of his chair as
he once again pictured her as she had looked in her
bedchamber earlier: her hair slightly dishevelled, her
cheeks flushed from the tears she had cried, her eyes
dark with hurt, the swell of her breasts softly rising
and falling as she breathed, her arms long and slen-

hours, stood out in stark relief against that darkness. The unfastened shirt at his throat revealed a hint of dark hair covering his muscled chest.

Her chin rose determinedly before she lost her nerve and turned on her heel and fled. 'Has Pelham retired for the night?'

Griffin continued to glower. 'I believe so, yes.'

She nodded. 'I waited upstairs in my bedchamber after my bath until I believed he might have done,' she informed him softly.

His eyes narrowed warily. 'Why?'

Now that she was here, face to face with this physically mesmerising man, Bea was starting to wonder that herself!

It had all seemed so simple up in her bedchamber earlier. She would take a leisurely bath, wait for the household to go to bed before then going downstairs to seek out Griffin, with the intention of tempting him into kissing her again. With the intention of showing him she most certainly was not *a mouse*. Here and now, faced with the sheer masculinity of the man, she felt decidedly less confident.

What did she possibly have to offer a man of such sophistication and self-confidence as him? A man, a duke, who only had to snap his elegant fingers to have any woman he chose?

In her present loss of memory, homeless, friendless state, absolutely nothing.

Her nerve completely failed her. 'I have been

lashes, easily noting the slightly fevered glitter in his eyes, and the flush high on those sharply etched cheekbones. There was a nerve pulsing in his tightly clenched jaw, and the width of his chest rapidly rose and fell as he breathed. 'I should like it very much if you did,' she insisted softly.

He eyed her impatiently. 'What are you doing?' he barked even as his hands came quickly from behind his back as she hurtled across the room and into his arms.

Her arms were about his waist as she burrowed into the comforting hardness of his chest. 'I feel so safe when you hold me in your arms, Griffin.'

Safe? Griffin echoed the word incredulously.

Bea felt *safe* when he held her?

It was the very *last* thing she was when his body reacted so viscerally to the feel of the warm softness of her body nestled so closely against it. He was a man of flesh and blood, not a blasted saint!

As the swell of his arousal testified.

Bea sighed her contentment. 'This is so very nice.'

His gaze sharpened with suspicion as she looked up at him. Was that a glint of mischief he could see in her eyes? A curve of womanly satisfaction to the fullness of her lips?

It was, damn it!

He pulled back slightly so that he could see her face more clearly; yes, he could definitely see challenge now in the darkness of her gaze, and her

'Then you are a reckless fool!' Griffin grated even as he pulled her into his arms and his mouth laid siege to hers.

Bea groaned her satisfaction as she gave herself up to the savagery of his kiss, eagerly standing on tiptoe as she moulded her body against his much harder one.

Her hands moved up his chest, feeling the soft hair visible there, lingering for several seconds, caressing that silkiness, as he moaned softly. She then slid her hands over the muscled width of his shoulders, her fingers becoming entangled in the darkness of the hair at his nape as the heat between them intensified and grew.

Bea whimpered low in her throat as Griffin now widened her stance to grind the hardness of his arousal into the inviting softness between her thighs, drawing her breath in sharply through her nose as he touched a part of her that caused the heated pleasure to course wildly through her veins.

She was lost in a maelstrom of emotions as his mouth continued to devour hers, even as his large hands restlessly caressed the length of her spine before settling on her bottom as he pulled Bea in even closer. The rhythmic stroking of his arousal now sent heated pleasure through the whole of her body; her nipples were full and aching, and between her thighs was swollen and warm.

Reckless fool or not, Bea didn't want Griffin to

His breath caught in his throat as she pulled his shirt free of his pantaloons before sliding it slowly up his chest. 'You really are playing with fire, Bea,' he gave her one last, growled warning.

She smiled up at him impishly. 'Then at least I shall be kept warm!' She pulled his shirt up, removing it completely. Her eyes were hot and devouring as she gazed at the muscled bareness of his chest before tentatively touching. 'You truly are magnificent, Griffin!' she breathed wonderingly as she smoothed her hands across his chest and over his nipples.

Her words, and her touch, caused Griffin's desire for her to rage out of control.

He had no memory of when a woman had last desired him for himself, and not because of his title or because she was being paid to want him. A sad state of affairs, indeed, but he had felt too raw after Felicity—

No!

He would not think of Felicity now.

Why should he think of her when there had been such an impenetrable coldness to his wife? A coolness he already knew Bea did not share.

Bea was warm—so very warm. She was responsive. Even now the hard berries of her nipples throbbed heatedly against the soft pads of his thumbs. And the scent of her arousal teased and tempted his senses, a mixture of honey and earthy, desirable woman.

because he was, after all, a gentleman, even in his desire for her.

How lucky his wife had been to have such a considerate husband. To have such a wonderful man in love with her. To be so privileged as to possess the care and devotion of such a man.

The desire Griffin now felt for her might only be a shadow of the emotions he had once felt for his dead wife, but surely it was enough?

Bea would make it be enough!

She continued to look into his eyes rather than down at her own body as her hands moved down to take hold of her nightgown. She slowly drew the material up to reveal her calves, then her thighs. The blush deepened in her cheeks as she raised the garment to her waist and saw Griffin's eyes darken, his heated gaze fixed on the V of silky ebony curls between her thighs.

'Higher,' he encouraged tightly.

Bea's hands trembled as she slowly pulled her nightrail up over her waist and breasts, her legs starting to shake as she heard his harshly indrawn breath as she removed the garment completely, dropping it down beside her robe as she stood naked before him.

'How beautiful you are,' he murmured as he sank to his knees in front of her, his large hands cupping both her breasts as he drank in his fill before slowly leaning forward to suckle one of her aching and engorged nipples into the moist heat of his mouth.

He lightly caressed her waist as he slowly released her nipple from his mouth.

'Griffin!' She looked down at him, need shining brightly in the feverish glow of eyes.

He took a few seconds to enjoy the sight of her engorged nipple, so moist and red and swollen from his suckling, before his gaze moved lower, his hands now resting on her hips as he held her in place before him and gently nudged her legs apart with his knees.

She was so aroused. For him. Because of him. Because of her desire for him.

'Griffin?' Bea's voice quivered her uncertainty as she watched his long fingers gently part the ebony curls between her thighs before he once again lowered his head towards her.

He glanced up at her, so close now the warmth of his breath brushed softly against a part of her that felt swollen and aching. 'Do you trust me, Bea?' he prompted huskily.

'Of course I trust you.' If she did not trust Griffin, then she could never, would never, trust anyone again.

'Then trust me now.' He blew delicately against that swollen ache between her thighs, causing her to shudder and tremble with the pleasure of that caress. 'Do you like that?'

'Yes,' she groaned weakly, fingers now digging painfully into his muscled shoulders. Although Griffin seemed unaware of any pain.

Until she did explode, deep inside her, the intense pleasure radiating outwards as well as inwards until she lay weak and gasping.

'Wh—what was that?' she gasped weakly.

Griffin moved to lie beside her as he slowly licked her juices from his lips. 'The French call it *le petit mort*—the little death,' he translated huskily.

Bea certainly felt as if she had died and gone to heaven and she was sure that she had never experienced pleasure like it.

'The English refer to it as a climax, or an orgasm.' Griffin smoothed the hair back from the dampness of her brow.

'I— Does that—does that always happen to a woman when—when a man and woman are t-together?' she prompted shyly.

'Only if the man cares enough to ensure her pleasure, which sadly too many rarely do.' His jaw tightened. 'And if the woman allows herself to become excited or stimulated.'

Bea gazed up at him searchingly, detecting a bitterness beneath his tone and the sudden bleakness of his expression. She was too satiated, too lethargic to care at that moment as she lay unabashedly naked beside him. Modesty seemed a little silly when Griffin had not only looked at her most intimate of places, but had also licked and tasted her there.

All bitterness fled as he smiled down at her, his

arouse her, to ease his passage, she had screamed the first time he had penetrated her, until he had retreated again when her sobs had become too much for him to bear. The second time had been no better, nor the third, thus setting a pattern for their physical intimacy that had never changed.

Not that he intended to penetrate Bea. She was an unmarried lady, an innocent still, whether she believed it or not, and once inside her Griffin knew he would be unable to stop himself from spilling his seed.

No, far better that he should send Bea back to her bed before he returned to his own chamber, where he could douse himself in cold water! 'I believe you might sleep now if you were to return to your bed-chamber.'

Bea was sure that she would, her body having an unaccustomed lethargy, a feeling of fullness and satiation, and no doubt resulting from her orgasm.

But she did not feel like falling asleep. She did not want their time together to be over just yet, and there was still that intriguing bulge in Griffin's pantaloons to explore.

'May I please see?' She looked at him encouragingly.

His jaw tightened as he obviously waged his own inner battle. Quite what that battle was, Bea had no idea, but she knew that there was one from the stormy grey of his eyes and the clenching of his jaw.

touch me I am afraid I shall—I shall be unable to maintain control myself!' he bit out forcefully.

'You will climax?'

'Without a doubt I shall, yes!'

Bea gave a confused shake of her head. 'Why should you not, when I have already done so?' Her cheeks felt warm.

Griffin drew in a deep and controlling breath. 'You asked to see and I have shown you. Are you not fearful? Overwhelmed by my size?'

'If I am overwhelmed then it is at your magnificence,' she assured him softly. 'And, no, I am not in the least frightened. Why should I be when this is a part of you?' She touched him gently with her fingertips, incredulous at how soft his skin felt when he was obviously so fiercely hard.

He was steel encased in warm velvet, her touches becoming bolder still as Griffin made no further objection to her explorations, although the grinding of his teeth spoke of his inner fight to remain in control as her hand cupped him.

He drew his breath in sharply as Bea's other hand then moved to close about him, and, recalling how Griffin had made love to her, she began to lower her head with the intention of feeling him with her mouth, her tongue.

'No, Bea!' Griffin groaned weakly in protest even as his body burned for more of her touch.

'Will it hurt you if I do?'

his fingers digging painfully into her shoulders as he continued to gasp his pleasure.

The arousal of Bea's own body rose with each hot and pulsing jet of Griffin's release, heat engulfing her as she climaxed for a second time, adding her own groans of completion to Griffin's.

to add to that uncertainty by taking such a socially inept man as her husband!

But should he at least insist she return to her own bedchamber before going to his?

Would she be happy with that, or would she want him to stay with her tonight?

Just thinking of lying beside her for the whole night, his body wrapped protectively about hers, was enough to cause his body to throb in anticipation of further lovemaking.

Lovemaking that should not—could not—happen again.

Tonight they had given each other pleasure with their mouths and hands, but if it was allowed to happen again how long before they—*he*—wanted more? Before he wished to possess Bea totally? How long before making love put them both at risk, so that marriage was no longer an option but a certainty?

Bea was warm and giving, yes, but Griffin did not need her to say the words to know that she would not want to tie herself to a man such as him for ever because of an unborn child.

Especially so when somewhere a man called Michael was awaiting her return.

'You are very quiet,' Bea said as she raised her head to look at him.

Griffin breathed in deeply before speaking. 'I was just thinking that—' He paused with a frown as there came the sound of a loud knocking. 'What the devil?'

she placed her trust, her naked self, so completely into the hands of another human being?

Certainly Griffin would not have been celibate in the years since his wife's death and yet he remained unencumbered by a second marriage, which would seem to imply that his affections had never been engaged in any of those liaisons.

Had Bea been foolish to believe that she was somehow different from the other women he had made love to, and that Griffin held some measure of affection for her?

Or was it just, in her determination to show Griffin she was not the mouse he believed her to be as well as her need to be with him, that she had deliberately chosen to *believe* that he cared for her?

Her memories of her own past might be seriously lacking at present, but still she knew instinctively that men were different from women, in that their physical desires were not necessarily accompanied by the same feelings of affection or love.

Love?

Did she *love* Griffin?

She certainly cared for him a good deal, and would be very sad to part from him when the time came, but was that love?

'Perhaps now that I have persuaded Pelham to go back to bed you will explain what the hell you are doing here!' she heard Griffin hiss fiercely from outside in the hallway.

'Bea, this is my friend Christian Seaton, the Duke of Sutherland,' Griffin introduced tersely.

The thing he had dreaded when he'd sent that letter to Maystone, that one of the Dangerous Dukes would hasten to Lancashire, had indeed come to pass. The question was, how much had Maystone imparted regarding the situation here?

He and Christian had a long-standing affection for each other, having attended Eton together, along with the other Dangerous Dukes, but even so Griffin knew that Christian was everything that he was not. Elegant. Charming. Fashionably dressed, no matter what the occasion.

Women had been known to swoon at Christian. Sensible women, matronly women, as well as the twittering debutantes who appeared in society every Season.

And Bea, Griffin noted somewhat sourly, had been unable to take her eyes off the man since he'd appeared in the doorway!

Was that *jealousy* Griffin felt towards his friend's easy charm and good looks?

Ridiculous.

And yet those feelings of bad humour persisted as he finished the introduction. 'Christian, this is my goddaughter, Beatrix.'

Bea offered Christian a shy smile. 'I prefer to be called Bea, Your Grace,' she invited huskily.

'I am pleased to meet you, Bea.' Christian nod-

of Sutherland seemed aware of the details of her current situation. Most especially so because she had never heard of the gentleman until his arrival a few minutes ago. 'Griffin?' she asked uncertainly.

Griffin moved to stand at her side. 'Christian is a trusted friend, Bea,' he assured her gruffly.

That might well be true. But was it not humiliating enough that Griffin knew of her circumstances, without the charmingly handsome Duke of Sutherland being aware of them too?

She turned to look at the man now. 'Do you know my true identity, sir?'

'I do,' he confirmed abruptly.

'And?' she prompted as he added nothing to that statement.

He winced. 'I have been instructed not to discuss the matter until Lord Maystone arrives.'

Bea stared at him incredulously. 'That is utterly ridiculous. Surely I have a right to know who I am? Why those things were done to me?' Two bright spots of angry colour burned in her cheeks as she glared at Christian Seaton.

'You have every right, yes.' He sighed. 'Unfortunately, I am not presently at liberty to discuss it.'

'Griffin?' Bea turned her angry gaze on him.

Griffin was as much at a loss as Bea. Except to know that Christian's silence on the subject, his added protection, implied Bea's situation was even graver than he had anticipated it might be. 'I believe

'And I have said that I have no wish to return to my bedchamber!'

'The two of us will talk again in the morning,' Griffin concluded firmly.

Bea glared first at Griffin and then at Sutherland, and back to Griffin. 'You are both mad if you believe I will calmly accept this silence until this Lord Maystone arrives!' She gathered up the bottom of her robe with an angry swish. 'I will give you both until morning to discuss the matter, and then I shall *demand* to know the answers!' She turned on her heel and marched angrily from the room.

'What a fascinating young woman,' Christian breathed as he gazed after her admiringly.

'You will keep your lethal charms to yourself where Bea is concerned.' Griffin was in no mood at present—or any other time, he suspected—to listen to or behold another man's admiration for Bea.

Christian gave him a long and considering stare. 'As you wish,' he finally drawled softly. 'In the meantime, perhaps you might care to explain to me just exactly what it was you were doing in the library with your "goddaughter" at this time of the night?'

Griffin felt his face go pale.

Hateful.

Hateful *and* impossible, Bea decided as she angrily paced the length and breadth of her bedchamber.

Both of them!

Would Christian Seaton, wickedly handsome, and so obviously a sophisticated gentleman of the world, have been able to tell, just from looking at the two of them, that she and Griffin had been making love together when he arrived?

Oh, dear Lord, could this night become any more humiliating?

Bea gave a muffled sob as she buried her face in the pillow, once again afraid. Of the knowledge of her past. Of what her future might hold.

Of having to leave Griffin.

'I would not care to discuss it, no,' Griffin answered the other man tightly as he moved to lift the decanter on his desk, pouring brandy into two of the crystal glasses before handing one to his friend. 'Who is she, Christian? And why all the secrecy?'

Christian took a grateful swallow of the amber liquid before answering him. 'We believe her name to be Lady Beatrix Stanton. She is nineteen years of age, and the unmarried daughter of the Earl and Countess of Barnstable. You will recall that both the Earl and his countess perished in a carriage accident last year? As for the rest...' He grimaced. 'The demand for secrecy is all Maystone's doing, I am afraid.'

Bea's name was Beatrix Stanton. She was the unmarried *Lady* Beatrix Stanton, Griffin corrected

'I am sorry, Griff, but I believe you are now crossing into the area where Maystone has demanded secrecy.' Sutherland grimaced.

Griffin's eyes widened. 'You are refusing to tell me who Bea's guardian is?'

The other man's mouth tightened. 'I am ordered not to tell you, Griff. There is a difference. This does not just involve the young lady you have claimed as your goddaughter,' he bit out harshly as Griffin looked set to explode into anger. 'The lives of other innocents are also at stake.'

Griffin stilled, eyes narrowed. 'What others?' he demanded. 'I always could pummel you into the ground, Christian,' he reminded grimly as the other man sipped his brandy rather than answer his question.

Sutherland sighed heavily as he relaxed back in the chair. 'Then you will just have to pummel away, I am afraid, Griffin, because I am not—'

'You are not at liberty to tell me,' Griffin finished grimly. 'Maystone believes Bea's life is still in danger?' he added sharply.

'It is the reason I have travelled here so quickly,' Christian confirmed.

Part of Griffin bristled at Maystone having doubted that he alone could protect Bea. Another part of him was grateful to have Christian's assistance.

If Bea truly was still in danger, then he welcomed any assistance in ensuring her safety.

riously engaged. It was…a mistake, an impulse, of the moment. She was upset, I attempted to comfort her, and the situation spiralled out of control. It will not happen again.'

'No?'

'No!' Even as he had made the explanation, and now the denial, Griffin knew that he was not being altogether truthful. With himself or Christian.

He *had* been attempting to comfort Bea earlier, but she had made it clear that she needed something else from him, something more.

Something he had been only too willing to give her.

And would willingly give time and time again if asked.

Bea, listening outside the study door, having cried her tears and decided to return down the stairs with the intention of demanding that Seaton give her the answers to her many questions, instead now felt as if her heart were breaking hearing Griffin describe their lovemaking as a mistake that he would not allow to happen again…

room, where he and Christian were already seated and enjoying breakfast. Her pallor did not in any way, though, detract from her fresh beauty, dressed as she was today in a pretty yellow gown that complemented her creamy complexion and gave an ebony richness to her hair.

Bea looked coolly across the table at him. 'How am I to tell, when my life has become nothing but a continuous nightmare from which I would rather awaken?'

Griffin scowled as he saw the corners of Christian's lips twitch with amusement as the other man obviously heard the sharp edge to Bea's reply.

A reply that implied she considered their love-making last night to be a part of that nightmare existence.

It had been Griffin's intention to apologise to her this morning at the earliest opportunity for the serious lapse in his behaviour and judgement but he now found himself bristling with irritation instead.

At the same time as he knew it was illogical of him to feel regret for his own actions, but feel offended when Bea expressed she felt the same way.

If only Christian were not here, perhaps he might have tried to explain to Bea *why* he regretted it.

'If you will both excuse me?' As if aware of Griffin's thoughts, Sutherland placed his napkin on the table before rising to his feet, an expression of studied politeness on his face as he bowed to them both.

'I have no objection if Griffin does not?' Christian still eyed him questioningly.

Bea bristled resentfully at the mere suggestion that it was any of Griffin's business what she chose to do after the conversation she had overheard between the two men last night. Griffin had dismissed not only her, but also their lovemaking, as a mistake that meant nothing to him.

'I believe I shall stroll in the garden, in any case,' she stated determinedly. 'If we should happen to meet, Your Grace—' she glanced coolly at Seaton '—then perhaps we might stroll along together.'

'Bea—'

'If you will excuse me, I believe I will go to my room and collect my bonnet.' Again Bea ignored Griffin as she turned on her heel and marched determinedly from the room, her head held high.

'As I remarked last night,' Sutherland mused softly as he watched her leave, Pelham following, at Griffin's discreet nod for the butler to do so, 'Bea is a fascinating young woman.'

'And as I replied, you are to stay away from her.' Griffin glared.

'Can I help it if she prefers my company to yours today?' the other man drawled dryly.

'This is not a laughing matter, Christian.'

'I could not agree more.' Sutherland sobered grimly. 'Will you accompany Bea on her walk, or shall I? In any case, she should not be left to stroll

seen no one who doesn't belong here in the immediate area.'

The other man raised blond brows. 'Then perhaps the people in question are not strangers?'

Not strangers? Did that mean that the person, or people, who had abducted and harmed Bea might belong to the village of Stonehurst? That one of his own neighbours, possibly one of the ones whom he had visited just days ago, might be in cahoots with Jacob Harker, whom Griffin was still convinced had been Bea's jailer?

It did make more sense if that were the case, than that Jacob Harker had randomly chosen one of Griffin's own woodcutters' sheds on the estate in which to hide and then mistreat Bea.

But which of his neighbours could have been involved in such infamy? One of those social-climbing couples he had visited, and whose only interest had appeared to be to show off their marriageable daughters to him? Or the jovial Sir Walter? One of Griffin's own tenants? Someone who actually worked here in the house?

If it was the latter, then surely there would have been another attempt to silence Bea before now.

'I believe you must be the one to accompany Bea this morning, Christian,' he murmured softly as he heard her coming back down the stairs after collecting her bonnet. 'While you are gone I will ride over to visit a neighbour who has invited me to come and

'Women in general are complicated, I have recently been reminded.' Griffin grimaced.

The other man smiled. 'Have no fear, Griff, between the two of us we will ensure that no harm comes to your Bea.'

'She is not my Bea,' Griffin bit out harshly.

'No?'

'No,' he repeated emphatically.

No, nor would she ever be. Once Bea's memory was restored to her, and this business was over with, she would be able to return to whatever family she had left.

And the mysterious Michael.

'You really should not hold Griffin responsible for this present situation, you know,' the Duke of Sutherland remarked quietly, Bea's gloved hand resting lightly on his arm as the two of them strolled about the garden together.

No, Bea did not know.

She was grateful to Griffin for all he had done for her this past week, but that kindness could not excuse his deliberate silence over her identity. He did know now, she felt sure of it.

Nor could she forgive him for so easily dismissing the intimacies between them last night when he had spoken with Seaton.

Most of all she could not forgive him for that!

Their lovemaking had been beautiful. A true giv-

He nodded. 'I do not believe I am being indiscreet by revealing that Griffin was placed in the school by his father when he was only eight years old. He was not a cruel man, merely elderly, and had been widowed since Griffin's birth. He did not, I believe, know quite what to do with his young son and heir, other than to place him in the competent hands of first a wet-nurse, then a nanny, and, finally, school.'

'But how lonely that must have been for Griffin!' Bea frowned at the thought of that lonely little boy, motherless, and sent away from the company of his father at such a tender age.

'Just so.' Seaton grimaced. 'We others did not join him until four years later. There were five of us altogether, all heir to the title of Duke. We were, and still are, a close-knit bunch. We became our own family, I believe, and have always looked out for each other,' he added enigmatically.

Bea's interest quickened. 'Then you also knew his wife?'

'I did, yes.' Seaton's expression became blandly unrevealing.

She nodded. 'Griffin loved her very much.' And no wonder, if he had led such a lonely childhood as Seaton had described. Griffin must have been so gratified to have someone of his own at last. Someone to love and want him.

Blond brows rose. 'Did he tell you that?'

'Well, no.' Bea frowned. 'But surely it is obvious?'

closest friends had all—perhaps still?—worked in some way for the Crown.

It would explain so much about Griffin. The deft and efficient way in which he had dealt with her own unexpected and unorthodox appearance into his life. The fact that he had connections in London, like Lord Maystone, whom he might call upon discreetly to help him in discovering her identity.

It was perhaps also the reason Griffin had never married again; working secretly for the Crown could no doubt be a hazardous occupation, even in times of peace, as it now finally was. Already a widower, he was not a man who would allow his own actions to risk making his wife a widow.

Could that be the reason he was choosing to discourage her own affections?

No, it was more likely that Griffin simply did not feel that way about her.

But the rest of it?

Oh, yes, knowing Griffin she could well believe the rest of it.

Griffin was above all a man of honour, of deep loyalties, and once that loyalty had been given she had no doubt that he would never betray it. For anything or anyone.

'I see.' She nodded slowly.

'I hope that you do.' Sutherland gave a slight inclination of his head. 'Griffin is a good man, and I

that they might continue their walk about the gardens together.

But that did not mean that Bea did not continue to think of their conversation. For her heart to ache for the lonely little boy Griffin must once have been. For the sad and lonely widower he must also have been these past six years since he'd lost his wife.

For Bea to feel ashamed of her harshness towards him this morning, when she had spoken and treated him so coldly.

As no doubt the wily Duke of Sutherland had intended her to feel…

'Yes, Bea?' Griffin eyed her warily as she appeared in the doorway of the library, where he currently sat alone, drinking whisky and contemplating the unpleasantness of his visit to Latham Manor this morning.

She hesitated. 'I am not interrupting anything?'

'Only my thoughts,' he acknowledged dryly.

Lady Francesca had arrived back at Latham Manor the previous evening, and, as Griffin had quickly learnt, her acerbic tongue had not been in the least tempered by having spent the Season in London, followed by several weekend parties on her leisurely journey back into Lancashire.

'Thoughts I can well do without,' he added dismissively as he stood up and indicated that Bea

Griffin tensed as he raised his gaze sharply to look searchingly at Bea. 'An apology for what?'

She sighed. 'I believe I was—unfair to you, both last night and this morning. The Duke of Sutherland was kind enough to explain a little about the restraints put upon the two of you, in regard to revealing my true identity.'

Griffin felt a certain satisfaction in hearing her still refer to Christian formally; he did not think he could have born to suffer through listening to Bea referring to the other man in a familiar way.

He was not so pleased with the rest of the content of her apology, however. 'And how did Christian do that?'

Bea sensed the reserve in Griffin's tone. 'His Grace was not in the least indiscreet, Griffin,' she hastened to reassure. 'He merely helped me to understand that there is more involved in all of this than my own personal wants and needs.'

'Indeed?'

Griffin sounded even more cool and remote when all she had wished to do was settle the unease that now existed between the two of them.

She had not forgotten overhearing his dismissal of their lovemaking last night, nor would she, but Christian Seaton *had* helped her to understand that there was a much broader picture to this situation, one that required she put her personal feelings of hurt to one side.

He stood up restlessly. 'I am trying, in my obviously clumsy way, to put things right between us. To—to—I wish to have the old Bea returned to me!' he rasped.

Bea had to harden her heart to the frustration she could hear in his voice, knowing she could never again feel so at ease in his company after the events of last night. Not because she regretted them in the slightest, because she did not. It was overhearing Griffin voice *his* regrets over those events that now constrained her.

He loomed large and slightly intimidating over the chair in which she sat. 'Bea, if I could turn back the clock, and make it so that last night had never happened, then I would,' he assured her with feeling. 'I would do it, and gladly!'

Bea felt the sting of tears in her eyes. She had not thought that Griffin could hurt her more than he already had, but obviously she had been wrong.

A numbing calm settled over her. 'If anyone is responsible for the events of last night, then it is me. You did warn me against proceeding, but I refused to listen. You are not to blame, Griffin,' she repeated firmly as she stood up. 'I have made my apology, now if you will excuse me?'

'No!' Griffin reached out to grasp hold of her arms as she would have brushed past him. 'No, Bea, I will not, I cannot let you leave like this. Beatrix Stanton!' he bit out grimly as she kept her face turned

Chapter Eleven

'**D**id you not consider how dangerous it could be to tell an amnesiac the truth so bluntly?'

'Obviously I know now.' Griffin turned to scowl his impatience at Christian as the other man restlessly paced the length of the library and back.

Griffin sat beside Bea on the chaise, where he had placed her tenderly just minutes before, and now held one of her limp hands in his.

The other man frowned. 'I thought we had agreed last night that we would not tell Bea anything until after Maystone's arrival?'

'*You* agreed that with Maystone, not I,' Griffin growled. 'And in making that agreement the two of you seem to have forgotten that Bea is a person not an object, and that she at least had the right to know who she is.'

Christian ceased his pacing before slowly nodding. 'I apologise.' He grimaced. 'You are right, of course.'

Griffin raised surprised brows. 'I am?'

'You misunderstand the situation, Christian.' Griffin gave a shake of his head. 'Bea is grateful to me for my part in her rescue; that is all.'

Christian now eyed him pityingly. 'You are a fool if you believe that to be all it is.'

His eyes glittered in warning. 'I am not having this conversation, Christian.'

'Why on earth not? Griffin,' he continued in a reasoning tone, 'it is wrong of you to allow the events of the past to dictate how you behave now.'

'It is none of your affair, Christian.'

The other man continued to eye him in exasperation for several moments more before nodding abruptly and changing the subject. 'Do you think it possible that revealing Bea's name to her may have triggered a return of her memories?'

'Why?' Griffin looked at his friend through narrowed lids. 'What is it that she knows, Christian, that is of such importance Maystone sent you here almost immediately he received my letter? Why does he need to come here himself?'

Christian straightened. 'I have allowed that Maystone and I were wrong in deciding to keep Bea's identity from her until he arrives, but I will not concede any further than that. Please try to understand, Griff,' he added persuasively. 'I assure you Maystone is not being difficult, but he has his own reasons for remaining cautious. Reasons I cannot as yet confide.'

'I believe *I* might perhaps shed at least a little

again swirling as some of the memories still danced elusively out of her reach.

'Of course.' Griffin stood up immediately to cross the room to where the decanter and glasses sat upon his desk top, pouring the dark amber liquid into a glass before returning.

Bea had managed to sit up completely in his absence, slippered feet placed firmly on the floor, her hands shaking slightly as she accepted the glass before taking a reviving sip of the drink.

So many of her memories had now returned to her. Her parents' death the previous winter was the most distressing.

They had been such a happy family. Her parents were still so much in love with each other, and it was a love that had included rather than excluded their only child. So much so that they had been loath to accept any of the offers of marriage Bea had received that previous Season, determined that their daughter should find and feel the same deep love for and from her husband. They wished for her to find a happy marriage, such as they had enjoyed together for twenty years.

After their sudden deaths her guardianship had been given over to her closest male relative— Oh, dear Lord!

'Bea?' Griffin prompted sharply.

She looked up at him with pained eyes. 'Please be patient with me, Griffin. It is such a muddle still

any idea what it is that my abductors thought I might know.'

'No idea at all?' Seaton looked disappointed.

'No,' she confirmed heavily before turning to Griffin. 'However, Griffin, I am now aware of who my—'

'Lord Maystone, Your Grace.' Pelham had appeared unnoticed in the library doorway, quickly followed by the visitor.

Bea turned in surprise to look at the visitor as he strode hurriedly into the room without waiting for Griffin's permission to do so.

Lord Maystone was a man possibly aged in his mid to late fifties, and he appeared a little travel-worn, as might be expected. But he was a handsome man despite his obviously worried air, with his silver hair and upright figure.

Bea did not recall ever having seen or met him before this evening.

Griffin scowled darkly as he looked across the room at Maystone. 'It's about time you arrived and gave an explanation for this whole intolerable situation!' He turned all of his considerable anger and frustration onto the older man.

'Griff—'

'I will thank you not to interfere, Christian.' Griffin eyed his friend coldly.

'I believe Aubrey might be in need of some refreshment before we do or say anything further?' Christian pointedly reminded Griffin of his manners.

'Griffin?' Bea prompted pointedly, her attention and concern all on Aubrey Maystone.

Griffin caught the mocking glint in Christian's eyes as he moved to pour Maystone a brandy. As if the other man found Bea's somewhat imperious behaviour towards him amusing. Or, more likely, Griffin's reaction to it...

As far as he was concerned, this situation had already caused more than enough of an upset between himself and Bea, and he did not intend to tolerate much more of it. His scant patience had come to an end.

He moved stiffly away to stand before the window once he had handed over the glass of brandy to Maystone. 'I assure you, I am nowhere near as tolerant of this situation as Bea!'

'Griffin!'

'Griff!'

He scowled as he was simultaneously reprimanded by both Bea and Christian.

'Rotherham is perfectly within his rights to feel irritated by my request for secrecy.' Lord Maystone sighed deeply once he had swallowed a large amount of the brandy in his glass and some of the colour had returned to his cheeks. 'It is—' He broke off as Pelham returned with a tray carrying the second decanter of brandy, the pot of tea also in evidence. 'This is something of a lengthy tale, so I suggest we all make ourselves comfortable by sitting down and

'I am, yes.' Bea gave Griffin a sideways glance from beneath her lashes.

Maystone nodded. 'Then I must also reveal that both Rotherham and Sutherland have for some time kindly assisted me in my less public work for the Crown.'

'I am aware of that also, Lord Maystone.' Bea turned away from Griffin's scowl to give the older man a reassuring smile. 'I am sure that you can appreciate it was necessary, for my own protection, that I be made aware of it?'

'I am sure Griffin acted only for the best.'

'I was the one to inform Lady Bea of the reason for my hurried presence here, not Griffin,' Seaton interjected decisively.

Lord Maystone's brows rose. 'Indeed?'

'Could we just get on with this?' Griffin glared his impatience over the delay; he just wanted to get this whole sorry business over and done with.

So that he might talk alone with Bea.

So that he might apologise for upsetting her earlier.

So that he might *be* alone with her.

He had always enjoyed Christian's company in the past, and the same was true of Aubrey Maystone, but here and now they both represented a deepening of that barrier between himself and Bea that he found so intolerable.

'Of course.' The older man sighed as he turned

he could have no idea that Bea had suffered a temporary loss of her memories following the trauma of her abduction and frightening escape.

Nor did Griffin believe, with the information Christian had imparted to him, that Harker was acting upon his own initiative.

One, or perhaps more than one, other person was most assuredly in control of these events.

'My concern was not for myself,' Bea now assured Lord Maystone huskily; in truth, her present alarm was all on Griffin's behalf upon learning that he had been involved in the risky business of preventing a plot to assassinate the Prince Regent.

That Griffin might have been killed before she'd even had opportunity to meet him.

'What a sweet and caring child you are.' Lord Maystone smiled at her warmly before that smile turned regretful. 'Which only makes my guilt all the deeper regarding my own involvement in your sufferings— Not her abduction, Rotherham.' He frowned as Griffin tensed in his chair. 'Do give me a little credit, please. I was not even aware of Lady Bea's abduction until after you wrote and told me of it.'

'But you most certainly knew something was afoot,' Griffin put in testily. 'As is someone else; Bea's real guardian must also have been aware of it when she completely disappeared.'

'Griff—'

ents and his family, for the sole intention of using the threat of taking his life as leverage in gaining access to certain information that might, indeed undoubtedly would, help in their cause against the Crown.'

'Good God!' Griffin breathed softly.

Maystone looked up at him with bloodshot eyes. 'That child is my grandson.'

Griffin closed his eyes in shame for his earlier rebukes and the anger he had shown towards Maystone since his arrival.

The man's grandchild had been abducted, his life threatened.

As Bea's had.

No wonder Maystone had added two and two together—his grandson's abduction followed by Griffin informing him Bea had suffered the same fate—and come to the conclusion of four!

Especially so when Griffin had stated in his letter to Maystone that there was a possibility that Jacob Harker, known to have been involved in the plot to assassinate the Prince Regent, and a man who just a few weeks ago had been seen in the area of Stonehurst, might have been involved in Bea's abduction and imprisonment. Bea's memory of the man's name being Jacob had, as far as Griffin was concerned, confirmed that suspicion, which he had also stated in his letter to Maystone. That had obviously caused both Sutherland and Maystone to travel so quickly to Stonehurst.

which you can maintain that loyalty and still rescue your grandson?'

'We must respect Lord Maystone's views, Bea.' Griffin had easily seen and recognised that stubborn set to her mouth as the precursor to her frankly stating her own views on the subject.

'Why must we?' She stood up abruptly, those flashing blue eyes now including him in her anger. 'We are talking of a little boy, Griffin,' she added emotionally. 'A little boy who has been taken from his parents, from all that he loves. He must be so frightened. So very, very frightened.' Her hands were so tightly clasped together her knuckles showed white, as she so obviously lived through memories of her own abduction and imprisonment. When she had suffered through that same fear of death, of dying.

'You must remain calm, Bea.' Griffin quickly crossed the room to clasp her clenched hands within his own.

'I do not see why.' Tears swam in those pained blue eyes as she looked up at him. 'Consider how you would feel, Griffin, if the child who had been taken were your own? How you would feel if your own son had been snatched from—?' She broke off as there came the sound of choking, both of them turning to look at Aubrey Maystone.

Just in time to see him fall back against the chaise, a hand clutching at his chest, his face as white as snow.

her comfortingly. 'The man has been beside himself with worry, and I have no doubts that this prolonged strain, and these added days of travelling, are the only reason for his collapse tonight.'

'Why did he not confide in me?' Griffin gave a pained frown. 'We could all have assisted in searching— No,' he guessed heavily. 'I am sure one of the kidnappers' demands was for Maystone's silence on the affair.'

Indeed, Griffin had thought of Bea's accusation prior to Maystone's collapse: How *would* he have felt if it had been his child who had been taken? Would he have turned England upside down in an effort to find his son? Or would he have done what Maystone had done, and suffered in silence himself rather than put the child's life in jeopardy?

If he had known Bea prior to *her* abduction, would he have been able to stay silent when she was taken, in the hopes it might save her life?

The answer to that was he had already been doing exactly that for this past week.

As had the man Michael for whom she had cried out in her sleep? The man whom she must surely now remember?

Perhaps that was what she had been about to tell Griffin earlier, when Maystone had arrived and interrupted her.

Christian stood up restlessly. 'Maystone decided that, as you were leaving to follow up the rumour of

'It certainly will be once Bonaparte is safely delivered and incarcerated on—' Sutherland broke off abruptly, giving an impatient shake of his head. 'At the moment there are legal moves afoot by Bonaparte's followers, to ensure that he remains in England. That is something the Crown and government simply cannot allow to happen.'

'Understandably,' Bea acknowledged softly.

Christian grimaced. 'That legal process has been deliberately delayed, for obvious reasons, so that— Suffice it to say that, for the moment, for the matter of a few more days only, it is still possible for Bonapartists in England to foil the arrangements made for his incarceration. After which they are no doubt hoping to see him safely returned to France, at which time a civil war will once again break out, allowing Bonaparte to prevail through the ensuing chaos.'

'But surely the French people have already spoken, by accepting the return of their King?' Bea did not pretend to know a great deal about politics, few ladies of her age did, but even she did not believe that the usurper Napoleon could reign without the will of the majority of the people.

Sutherland gave a rueful shake of his head. 'A number of French generals have spoken, as has the British government and its allies, but they alone are responsible for the Corsican's complete defeat, and returning Louis to his throne. Napoleon's charisma

return him to his parents and grandfather, before it was indeed too late.

Just the thought of an eight-year-old boy suffering the same cruel imprisonment that she had was beyond bearing.

'Griffin?' she appealed.

Griffin had never felt as impotent as he did with Bea looking up at him so trustingly. As if she believed he was capable of solving this situation when Maystone and Christian had been unable to in the past three weeks.

But he dearly *wanted* to deserve that look of complete trust, to be the hero that Bea believed him to be.

He turned to Christian. 'Have you and Maystone made any progress at all?'

Christian grimaced. 'We have arrested several more people involved in the original assassination plot, but all claim to know nothing of the kidnapping of Maystone's grandson. Consequently they did not have any information on where the boy is being held. Your information of Lady Bea's abduction, so similar to that of Maystone's grandson, is the first real indication we have had that mistakes are being made. Desperation is setting in, and when that happens...'

'The whole begins to unravel,' Griffin finished with satisfaction.

'But I have told you both that I do not know why I was taken! That I do not know anything.' Bea hesitated. 'That is not completely true. I now know *where*

ant and jovial enough fellow, but otherwise— You already knew of this connection, Christian, and said nothing?' he accused, recalling how he had sensed his friend's air of reservation when they had spoken of Sir Walter earlier.

The other man gave a frustrated shake of his head. 'The fact that Lady Bea is his ward does not make Sir Walter guilty of any more than negligence at the moment, in having failed to report her as missing. And there are often other reasons than kidnapping for a young lady's sudden disappearance,' he added dryly.

Griffin turned back to Bea. 'You said your aunt accompanied you to this house party?'

'Yes,' she confirmed hesitantly.

That Lady Francesca Latham, always so cold and mocking, might be involved in intrigue and kidnapping, Griffin certainly *could* believe.

Especially so, when only this morning she had told him herself that her niece had decided to stay with friends rather than immediately accompany her aunt to her new home to Lancashire.

Unless...

Unless he was allowing his own dislike of Lady Francesca, and her past influential friendship with his wife, to colour his judgement?

The possible explanation for Lady Francesca's lie, as to her niece-by-marriage's whereabouts, might be that she was under the same warning of silence as

It was ridiculous of him to feel wary of her. Admittedly, she was still hurt at overhearing his rejection of their lovemaking. But she could never be truly angry with Griffin. She cared about him too much for that to ever be true. He could not be blamed for not having that same depth of feeling for her.

'What are—?'

'Are you—?'

They both began speaking at once, both stopping at the same time.

Bea looked across at Griffin shyly as he politely waited for her to speak first. 'What are we to do next, do you think?'

'Regarding the recovery of Maystone's grandson?'

'What else?' she prompted softly.

What else indeed, Griffin acknowledged, knowing it was ridiculous of him to think that Bea would have any interest in discussing the subject of their closeness last night when she now knew exactly who she was.

Who Michael was.

It irked that as yet she had still made no mention of the other man in her life.

Out of embarrassment and awkwardness, perhaps, because of their own closeness last night?

Bea need have no qualms in that regard where Griffin was concerned; what had happened between the two of them had been madness. A wonderful sensual madness, but it had been madness nonetheless.

He seemed to be fighting a constant battle within himself where she was concerned. The need to be close to her, to make love to her again, was set beside the knowledge that he did not have that right. That Bea belonged to another man.

Even if she had chosen not to speak to him of that man, as yet.

How could she, when he had taken such liberties? When just to think of the two of them together last night must now cause her immeasurable embarrassment and guilt?

No, better by far that he respect her silence, and the distance now between them, rather than cause them both further embarrassment.

'Griffin, do you think that I should go to—?'

'No!' he protested violently.

Her eyes opened wide at his vehemence. 'You do not know what I was about to say.'

'Oh, but I do,' he assured her dryly. 'You have shown yourself to be both a courageous and resourceful woman this past week.'

'I do not believe that to be true.' She shook her head sadly.

'Oh, but it is,' Griffin countered. 'You are very determined. What's more you have refused to allow fear to dictate your movements. Consequently it is not in the least difficult for me to reason that you are thinking of offering yourself up as human bait, by going to your uncle and aunt's home in the hope

in possession of knowledge wanted by his kidnappers, as Bea apparently had.

'You really have no idea of what it is you might have overheard to cause your abduction?'

'None at all.' She gave a pained grimace. 'As far as I recall, it was just a weekend party, with the usual bored group of people attending.'

Griffin wished he dare ask if Michael had been one of those people, but again knew it would not be fair to place Bea in such a place of awkwardness. 'We will find Maystone's grandson, Bea, have no fear,' Griffin stated with determination. 'And if anyone is going to visit the Lathams then it will be me,' he added grimly.

'But would it not look suspicious if you were to visit them again so soon?'

He smiled tightly. 'Not if my purpose was to make Sir Walter an offer for his new hunter. He will refuse, of course, and have the satisfaction of owning a piece of horseflesh he believes coveted by his neighbour.'

'You must be terribly good at the secret work you do for the Crown,' Bea murmured ruefully. 'That is what you and the Duke of Sutherland do for Lord Maystone, is it not?'

'We should not speak aloud of such things, Bea.'

'But why do you do it, Griffin?' She looked up at him in confusion. 'Why have you chosen to deliberately put yourself in danger?'

It had begun as a way for him to evade thoughts

Bea *cared*!

She cared very much what happened to Griffin.

Now and in the future.

Even if he did not want or need her concern.

'That is unfortunate—Your Grace!' She turned concernedly to the Duke of Sutherland as he appeared in the doorway. 'How is Lord Maystone feeling now?'

He stepped into the room. 'He wishes to speak with both of you now, if that is convenient?'

'Why?' Griffin eyed the other man suspiciously.

Sutherland looked grim. 'Best you speak to Maystone, Griff.'

Griffin had a fair idea of what Aubrey Maystone wished to discuss with him—at this point in time the older man was feeling desperate enough to go to any lengths to achieve the return of his grandson.

Even suggesting, as Bea had already done, that her immediate return to the Lathams' home might bring forth the breakthrough in this impasse that was so sorely needed.

Bea could not bear to be the cause of contention between Griffin and the gentlemen, who were obviously two of his closest friends. 'It is no more than I offered to do myself just minutes ago, Griffin,' she reminded softly.

'And if you recall I turned down that offer. Unequivocally!' he came back fiercely.

'But surely you can see it is the only course of action that makes any sense?' she reasoned. 'I will go to Latham Manor, having travelled from my friend's house under the kind protection of the Duke of Sutherland. At which time, my aunt and uncle will then either react with gladness at my safe return after my abduction, and so proving their innocence. Or they will both sincerely thank the Duke of Sutherland for having safely returned me from my visit with friends, and we will know that in all probability my aunt has lied. It all makes perfect sense to me.'

'It makes *no* sense to me!' Griffin bit out as he ran an exasperated hand through his hair.

'But—'

'It is far too dangerous, Bea,' he ground out harshly as he continued to glare down at her. 'Added to which, I absolutely forbid it!'

She sat back in surprise, not only at the fierceness of Griffin's emotions, but also because he felt he had the right to forbid her to do anything.

Admittedly he had been claiming to be her godfather and guardian this past week, as a means of ex-

perfectly safe under the protection of the Duke of Sutherland.'

That was one of Griffin's main objections to the plan!

Besides the obvious one of Bea deliberately placing herself in the path of danger.

Whether either of the Lathams were involved in her abduction or not, Bea's reappearance at their home would still leave her vulnerable to the people who had been responsible. To Jacob Harker, at the very least.

Besides which, if anyone was to act as Bea's protector then it should be him. In this particular situation that was an impossibility, when the Lathams lived but a mile away from Stonehurst Park, and he was supposed to be unacquainted with the Lathams' niece. And if Griffin could not be at her side, once she was returned to the uncertainty as to the innocence of the inhabitants of Latham Manor, then he could not, in all conscience, approve of Bea going there either.

Or bear the thought of her spending so much time alone with Christian.

Griffin knew his own nature well enough to realise he could be taciturn and brusque, and that his looks were not, and never would be, as appealing as Christian's. Just as he knew Bea could not help but be charmed by the man, as so many other women in

It was impossible, facing the three gentlemen as she was, for Bea to miss the knowing look that passed between Seaton and Lord Maystone, even if she did not quite understand it.

'By all means I will accompany you to the library, Griffin. Gentlemen.' She nodded politely to Sutherland and Maystone. 'But be aware, Griffin,' she added as he moved to politely open the door for her so that she might precede him out of the bed-chamber, 'I have no intention of allowing myself to be bullied. By you or anyone else,' she warned as she swept past him and out into the hallway.

Was it even sane of him, Griffin wondered as he had to hold back a smile as he accompanied Bea down the curved stairs to the library, to feel both admiration and frustration for her at one and the same time?

Admiration for the way in which she had conducted herself just now.

And frustration with the light of determination he had seen so clearly in her eyes as she gave him that set-down.

'I am aware our conversation was interrupted earlier, Bea,' he remarked as he closed the library door firmly behind them. 'But nevertheless, I cannot have left you in any doubt as to my disapproval of this scheme.'

Bea faced him as she stood in the middle of the

week by tending my cuts and bruises and feeding and clothing me.'

Griffin drew back as if Bea had struck him. Indeed, it felt as if she had just done so. 'That was an unforgivable thing for you to say, Bea.'

It was, Bea knew that it was. It was just that she'd felt so disconnected from Griffin since Christian Seaton's and Lord Maystone's arrival. As if the closeness the two of them had shared this past week had been completely rent asunder by the arrival of his other visitors.

She *missed* Griffin.

As she missed their previous closeness. Their conversations. Their bantering and occasional laughter. Their lovemaking.

But that was still no reason for her to have been so mean to Griffin just now.

She bowed her head in shame. 'I apologise, Griffin.' She looked up at him, tears blurring her vision. 'This is just such an awful situation for everyone, and I cannot bear the thought of that little boy being all alone, and suffering as I did. I want to *do* something to help him, Griffin.'

Griffin was well aware that she felt as impotent as he did over this situation. But, still, he could not bear the thought of her once again being placed in danger, and this time by a decision consciously made.

He knew he looked defeat in the face because of

The two of them remained looking at each other for several long moments, before Bea broke the connection as she sternly reminded herself of the conversation she had overheard last night between Griffin and his friend. She must not make the mistake again of thinking that his kindness towards her, his concern for her welfare, was anything deeper than that of a man who cared deeply for others—hence his work for the Crown these past years—even if he did not care to show it in the often stern exterior he presented to the world at large.

She released his hands before stepping away. 'I shall need to go up to my bedchamber and pack what few belongings I now have. I shall have to give the excuse to my aunt and uncle that, having accepted the Duke of Sutherland's protection for the journey, the rest of my luggage will be arriving later by carriage,' she added with a frown.

Griffin still believed this whole concept, of Bea going to Latham Manor, was fraught with the possibility of mistakes being made, of someone getting hurt. Possibly Bea herself. Mistakes she, or Griffin, or even Christian, would not have any control over.

Which was not to say Griffin did not intend to find some way in which he might watch over her himself.

'Do not scowl so, Griffin!' Bea advised teasingly the following morning as she sat in the coach op-

action to Bea's arrival. But this proposed visit to take another look at Sir Walter's hunter was the best that Griffin could come up with in the circumstances.

At least this way he might have opportunity to be formally introduced to Bea as Sir Walter's niece.

The irony of his eagerness now to be introduced to Sir Walter's niece, when he had not cared to meet the daughters and nieces of any of his other neighbours, was not lost on Griffin.

Nor was the possibility of Lady Francesca Latham being involved in the plot to secure Bonaparte's freedom.

Again Griffin questioned as to whether or not he was being influenced in this suspicion by his personal dislike of the woman. Lady Francesca had been far too much of a negative influence on his late wife, he suspected, in regard to their marriage, and him. And she'd enjoyed being so, if the mocking smiles Lady Francesca had so often given Griffin were an indication.

'Is that altogether wise, Griffin?' Christian frowned at Griffin's proposed visit to Latham Manor.

Wise, or otherwise, it was Griffin's intention to visit shortly after Christian and Bea had arrived. 'I shall be calling upon Sir Walter this morning.' He nodded.

'As you wish.'

'It is exactly as I wish.' Griffin gave another terse nod before stepping back and closing the carriage door.

has harmed so much as one hair upon Bea's head!' His teeth were clenched, a nerve pulsing in the tightness of his jaw.

The older man's expression softened. 'Perfectly understandable, when you are in love with her.'

'I— What?' Griffin looked at the other man incredulously. 'Of course I am not in love with Bea,' he denied harshly. 'I am concerned for her safety, that is all.'

'Of course you are.'

'I have had to suffer enough of Christian's sarcasm these past two days, and can quite well do without your adding to it!' Griffin scowled darkly.

The older man gave an acknowledging nod. 'It was not intended as sarcasm. Very well, I will say no more on the matter,' he acquiesced as Griffin continued to glare coldly across the carriage at him, before politely turning away to look out of the window at the trees lining the driveway.

Leaving Griffin alone with his thoughts.

Was he in love with Bea?

Of course he was not! The mere idea of it was preposterous, ridiculous.

Preposterous and ridiculous or not, was it possible that the feelings of jealousy, of possessiveness, which Griffin so often felt where Bea was concerned, might indeed be attributed to a growing affection for her?

No!

Chapter Fourteen

'The Duke of Rotherham and Lord Aubrey May-stone,' the Lathams' butler announced from the doorway of the salon in which Bea, Christian and Sir Walter Latham sat together drinking the tea she had recently poured for them.

She and Seaton had arrived at Latham Manor just thirty minutes previously, to be greeted enthusiastically by Sir Walter. And in such a manner as to indicate that the gentleman had no knowledge of Bea's abduction, but had in fact believed her to be visiting with friends.

Thus confirming Lady Francesca's guilt?

Unfortunately they had no answer yet as to whether that was indeed the case; Lady Francesca was out this morning, paying courtesy calls upon her neighbours.

The question now was whether or not Lady Francesca had actively lied to her husband regarding

ously slightly overwhelmed by the visit of yet more exulted company this morning.

'Latham.' Griffin nodded abruptly. 'My recently arrived guest, Lord Aubrey Maystone,' he introduced just as tersely, having eyes for no one else but Bea as she stood so still and composed across the room.

He could read nothing from her expression. Nor, as he glanced at Christian, did his friend give him any more than a shrug. One that seemed to imply frustration, rather than an indication that Christian had come any closer to learning the truth of this situation.

And the reason for that frustration soon became obvious as Sir Walter apologised because his wife, Lady Francesca, was presently not at home.

Lady Francesca's many absences from home might be perfectly innocent, but Griffin sensed, more than ever, that the woman had information that would give them the answers to the reason for Bea's abduction.

And might also lead to the whereabouts of Maystone's young grandson.

'More cups, if you please, Shaw,' Sir Walter instructed the butler once he had made Aubrey Maystone's acquaintance. 'I am sure you gentlemen must both already be acquainted with my guest, the Duke of Sutherland,' he continued jovially. 'And please allow me to introduce my ward, Lady Beatrix Stanton.'

Griffin nodded abruptly to Christian before he

ing and lovely, Your Grace,' Sir Walter acknowledged Griffin's compliment warmly.

Sir Walter appeared to be everything that was jovial and friendly, leading Bea to conclude that the chill of the house must have come from Lady Francesca.

During their months spent in London together Bea could not say that she had found the other woman to be of a type she might make into a bosom friend, but she had not found her to be unfriendly either. They were merely of a different age group, Lady Francesca nearing forty years of age, and Bea not yet twenty. Nor did Lady Francesca appear to possess the maternal instinct that might have drawn the two women closer together. That the Lathams' marriage was childless perhaps accounted for the latter.

Bea had no idea if she was merely being fanciful about her aunt-by-marriage, or allowing some of Griffin's obvious aversion to Lady Francesca to influence her own feelings towards the wife of her guardian.

No doubt they would all learn more upon that lady's return.

Bea felt a blush warm her cheeks as she became aware that the other three gentlemen in the room were now eyeing her and Griffin curiously. No doubt that was because Griffin still had a hold of her hand.

'May I pour you two gentlemen some tea?' She deftly slid her fingers from between Griffin's, be-

after receiving his cup of tea. 'You must allow us to see this fine horseflesh before we depart!'

Griffin took advantage of Sir Walter's fulsome praise of the other man's hunter in which to talk quietly with Bea. 'You are well?'

'Quite well, Your Grace,' she replied quietly as she handed him his tea. 'We only parted a short time ago,' she added even more softly.

Griffin put the cup and saucer down on the table beside him untouched as he kept the intensity of his gaze fixed upon Bea. 'And I have hated every moment of it!'

Bea gave him a searching glance, cautioning herself not to read too much into Griffin's statement; he could just be once again referring to the danger she had placed herself in rather than any deeper meaning.

Such as that he loved her as she surely loved him?

Bea had known it for a fact the moment the carriage had pulled away from Stonehurst Park earlier this morning. Had felt an ache in her heart such as she had never known before. An emptiness that could only be filled by Griffin's presence.

She loved him.

Not because she was grateful to him for having rescued her. Not because he had continued to protect her once he'd realised she had no idea who she was. Nor because they had made such beautiful love together.

departed Latham Manor. Just the thought of it was enough to make him clench his fists in frustration.

And he knew that feeling no longer had anything to do with thoughts of Bea remaining here in the company of Christian, and everything to do with—

'My dears, what a lovely surprise it is to see you all gathered together in my drawing room!' Francesca Latham swept into the room, blond head tilted at a haughty angle, blue eyes aglow with that mocking humour she so often favoured. 'I could barely credit it when Shaw informed me of our exulted company, Latham.' She moved to her husband's side. 'And I see dear Beatrix has also returned to us, in the company of the Duke of Sutherland.' That hard blue gaze now settled on Bea.

Griffin had stood up upon that lady's entrance. 'I am sure that must be as much of a pleasant surprise to you as it was to Sir Walter?'

'But of course.' That hard blue gaze now met his challengingly.

Griffin placed his clenched fists behind his back as he resisted the urge he felt to reach out and shake the truth from this woman.

Now that he was here he knew he could not leave here today until he knew whether this woman was Bea's friend or foe. And to hell with the politeness of manners! He was tired of this tedious social dance. He wished now only for the truth. 'You had perhaps not expected her to be here at all?'

of them had forgotten they were even in the company of others.

Implying a past rift much deeper than merely that he did not care for his neighbour's wife.

It appeared so to Bea. And she could think of only one reason why such tension might have arisen between two such handsome people. A past love affair that had not ended well.

The idea of Griffin having been intimately involved with Lady Francesca so sickened Bea that she could raise no further protest regarding the bluntness of his conversation.

'What on earth are you on about, Rotherham?' Sir Walter was red-faced with anger. 'You are either foxed or mad. Either way, you will apologise to my wife forthwith.'

'I will neither apologise nor retract my statement,' Griffin bit out harshly. 'You will answer the accusation, Lady Francesca. And you will do so now.'

'Remember my grandson, Griffin,' Lord Maystone cautioned softly.

'I have not forgotten,' Griffin assured him gruffly. 'As I have not forgotten the manner in which I found Bea, following her abduction and days of being held prisoner.' His voice hardened as he continued to look coldly at Lady Latham.

'Abducted? Held prisoner?' Sir Walter looked totally bewildered. 'But Beatrix has been staying with friends—is that not so, Francesca?'

She bared her teeth in a humourless smile. 'So Felicity liked to refer to me as, yes.'

'The two of you were lovers?'

'For many months.' Francesca Latham nodded with satisfaction.

'Francesca!'

'Oh, do be quiet, Walter,' his wife snapped dismissively as she gave him a contemptuous glance. 'We have not shared a bed for years, and now you know the reason why. I have always preferred my own sex,' she continued conversationally. 'Of course, Felicity did become a tad over-possessive and demanding, forcing me to end our association, but whoever would have thought the little ninny would have drowned herself for love of me? Quite tedious, I do assure you.' She gave an irritated shake of her head.

Bea had not been able to take her eyes off Griffin since her aunt had announced her past intimate relationship with his late wife.

Or to wonder if, as Seaton had implied yesterday, she had been mistaken in believing that the happiness Griffin had known in his marriage was the reason he had never remarried. He might have loved his wife, certainly, but he also seemed to have known that his wife's love had not belonged to him.

'But we digress,' Lady Francesca continued pleasantly. 'I take it the two other gentlemen here also wish to see justice done? As I thought.' She nodded at the silence that greeted her question. 'What hap-

seemed to have deflated into being a shell of himself in the past few minutes, his rosy cheeks now a sickly shade of grey.

'Do not tax your brain about it, Latham,' his wife dismissed mockingly. 'You would be far better to attend to your horses and your hounds.'

Latham attempted to rouse himself. 'You will answer me, madam. Who is this man Harker? What have you done that Rotherham now accuses you of being a traitor? It is something to do with that worthless half brother of yours, is it not?' He puffed angrily. 'I always knew he would be nothing but trouble.'

'Be silent, Latham!' His wife turned on him angrily, cheeks flushed. 'You are not fit to so much as speak my brother's name.'

'Half brother,' Sir Walter rallied defiantly. 'Sir Rupert Colville is only your half brother. A weak, lily-livered anarchist bent on bringing down the Crown.'

'I said be quiet!' Lady Francesca flew at him, hands raised, fingers bent into talons, her face an ugly mask.

Christian was closest to the couple, managing to grasp Francesca Latham about her waist and pull her back before she could reach her husband with those talons. Once she was in his grasp, he secured her more tightly by pulling her arms down and also holding them captive within his grasp as he stood behind her.

of such treatment. As such I will have no compunction in taking steps to silence you if you should give me reason to do so.'

'Do as you wish with me.' Francesca tossed her head unconcernedly. 'You may cut off the head of the snake but two more will grow in my place!'

'I do not believe for one moment that you are the head of this particular snake,' Griffin scorned. 'Nor your milksop brother, either. Neither of you is intelligent enough,' he added with hard derision. 'And I believe we will leave it to the Crown to decide whether or not to cut off both your heads.'

All the colour now drained from Francesca's cheeks. 'How can you remain loyal to such a man as the Prince Regent? A man who overindulges himself in every way possible, spending money he does not have on things he does not need, and to the detriment of his own people.'

'Oh, please, spare us your warped idea of patriotism!' Maystone dismissed. 'Also be assured, madam, that if my grandson is not returned to me unharmed, then I shall personally recommend the hardest sentence imaginable to the Prince Regent, for your crimes against both him personally and to England,' he added grimly.

Hatred now gleamed in those cold blue eyes. 'My brother should have disposed of the boy when I advised him to.'

'You will be quiet, madam!' Bea was shaking

contemptuously down his nose at Francesca. 'Where is Harker now?'

Francesca now seemed less defiant than she had a few moments ago. 'I presume he is in his hovel of a cottage, where I was forced to stay hidden during the week of Beatrix's imprisonment.'

Griffin's eyes widened. 'Harker lives in a cottage on my own estate?'

'His name is not Harker but Harcourt, and he is nephew to your own housekeeper,' Lady Francesca taunted.

Which explained, Griffin realised, why none in the area had reported seeing anyone suspicious or unknown to them. But did that also mean that Mrs Harcourt—?

'The old dragon has no idea of Jacob's political views, if that is what you are now thinking,' the blonde-haired traitor dismissed mockingly. 'Not that any of this matters now.' She took in everyone present in the room with one sweeping glance. 'You may rescue Maystone's grandson, arrest Jacob, Rupert and myself, do with us what you will. But, as I have stated, there are plenty of others who will happily take our place in securing Napoleon's freedom.'

'There are even more of us who will ensure they do not succeed,' Christian assured her grimly.

And no doubt Griffin would have to be one of them, he accepted heavily.

But once Maystone's grandson, Michael, was

Chapter Fifteen

Ten days later

'His Grace, the Duke of Rotherham, is here to see you, My Lady,' Shaw announced from the doorway of the drawing room in Latham Manor.

Bea's heart leapt in her chest at the news that Griffin was back in Lancashire, and she tensed as she looked up from the book she had been reading, as she sat in the window seat enjoying the last of the day's sunlight. 'You are sure the Duke is here to see me and not Sir Walter?'

Bea had not seen Griffin since Lady Francesca and her associate, Jacob Harcourt, had been placed in custody, and he had set off immediately for Worcestershire with Christian Seaton and Lord Maystone, their intention to liberate the latter's grandson from the home of Lady Francesca's half brother.

But not before it had been discussed and decided

Bea had resigned herself to not seeing Griffin again now that he was returned to London.

'His Grace asked for you specifically, My Lady,' the butler now assured her.

'Then you may show him in, Shaw.' Bea nodded.

She turned to quickly check her appearance in the mirror, her mouth having gone dry at thoughts of seeing Griffin again.

At thoughts of the heartache of the two of them meeting and greeting each other as if they were polite strangers.

When that was the last thing they were.

Or ever could be, as far as Bea was concerned.

Her heart almost jumped completely out of her chest as Griffin strode purposefully into the room, not pausing at the doorway but heading straight over to where Bea still stood near the window.

He looked so dark and handsome in his perfectly tailored black superfine, worn with a grey waistcoat and grey pantaloons, his black Hessians gleaming.

So dearly beloved.

'Your Grace.' Bea affected a curtsy, head bent so that Griffin should not see the tears of happiness glistening in her eyes just at the sight of him.

'Bea?' Griffin gave a dark frown as he reached out to place a hand beneath the softness of her chin and raise her face so that he might better see her expression.

of Bea's life after all, but Maystone's grandson, had come as even more welcome news. Michael had become a spectre in Bea's dreams only because of the warmth of her heart, her concern for a little boy she had believed to be orphaned, like herself.

That knowledge was the only thing that had kept Griffin sane as he'd dealt with all the other matters in need of his attention before he was free to return to Lancashire.

To return to Bea.

She looked so very beautiful. She was wearing a gown he had never seen before. No doubt one of her own, which had now been delivered from the house in Worcestershire. A gown of the palest blue silk that made her skin appear both pale and luminescent.

Her face appeared a little thinner than Griffin remembered, but that was surely to be expected after the upset of the previous weeks. And the added knowledge that it was her own aunt who was responsible for her abduction and the beatings she had received while held prisoner in the filthy woodcutters' shed.

One of Griffin's last instructions, before he'd departed Stonehurst Park in the company of Christian and Maystone ten long days ago, had been for that shed to be burnt to the ground. That not a single sliver of wood was to remain.

And now here was Bea, looking more beautiful to him than ever.

was enough to make her pulse beat faster. In fact, she would be surprised if Griffin could not hear the loud beating of her heart caused just by being near him again.

But it would be foolish of her to read any more into his visit to Latham Manor this morning than a courtesy call. To ensure that Bea was happy with her new guardian.

'I have stepped down from my work for the Crown, Bea.'

She was frowning slightly as she turned her head to look over her shoulder at him. 'You are perhaps tired of the intrigue and danger?'

Griffin gave a smile. 'I believe I would describe it more that I have found a reason to live.'

Bea's expression softened. 'I am so sorry for the things you have learnt about your late wife. It must have been such a shock to you.' She gave a shake of her head. 'I cannot imagine—'

'It was a relief, Bea,' he cut in firmly. 'Such a blessed relief,' he breathed thankfully. 'For years now I have blamed myself for the failure of my marriage, for not loving Felicity, or she me, so much so that she had preferred to take her own life rather than suffer to live with me another day. To finally know, even in such a way as I learnt the truth, that I was not responsible has caused me to hope—to dare to hope...'

Bea turned fully to face him, her gaze search-

digress.' He straightened. 'Something else I never talked of was the utter failure of my marriage.' He sighed. 'I realise the reason for that now. I accept it. But for those two reasons I have for years believed myself to be unlovable rather than just unloved.'

'Your friends all love you dearly,' she told him.

'Yes, I believe they do,' he acknowledged softly. 'But I had believed myself too dour, too austere, too physically overbearing, to deserve the love of any decent woman. I have lived my life accordingly, never wanting, never expecting, never *asking* for more than I had.'

The slenderness of Bea's throat moved as she swallowed. 'And that has now changed?'

'Completely,' Griffin stated without hesitation. 'Now I want it all. The wife. The children. The happy home. The love of the woman whom I love in return. My homes filled with vases of flowers,' he added ruefully.

Bea could barely breathe, so great was her own hope now that Griffin was talking to her of these things for a reason. 'And have you come here so that I might wish you well on this venture?'

'I want so much more from you than that, Bea,' he assured her firmly. 'I want, one day, for you to be my wife, the mother of my children, the mistress of my happy home, the woman who might love me as I have loved and continue to love you, and who will fill our homes with vases of flowers. I am more than

tinued to grow every moment of every day since. I *love* you, Griffin,' she repeated emotionally.

He looked uncertain, confused, two emotions Bea had never associated with this strong and decisive man. 'Are you sure you are not confusing gratitude with love?'

'Of course, I am grateful for your having rescued me, and caring for me even though you had no idea who I was or where I came from; what sort of woman would I be if I were not?' she dismissed indulgently. 'I am grateful for all that, but it is you that I love, Griffin. The man, the lover, not the rescuer. These last few days, of not knowing if I would ever see you again, have passed in a haze of agony for me,' she acknowledged huskily. 'I love you so much, Griffin, I cannot bear to be apart from you, even for a moment.'

It was so much how Griffin felt in regard to Bea. 'Will you marry me, Bea, and be my duchess?'

'I will marry you, and gladly, but so that we need never be separated again, not to become your duchess,' she answered him without hesitation.

Griffin grinned and gave a heartfelt whoop of gladness before he claimed her lips with his own.

'If you do not mind, I believe the wedding must be soon, my love,' he murmured indulgently some time later, as the two of them sat together upon the

friends will have to stand up with you, for I find I do not wish to wait either.'

Which was reason enough for Griffin to begin kissing her all over again…

* * * * *

Don't miss the next book in Carole Mortimer's dazzling DANGEROUS DUKES *duet:* CHRISTIAN SEATON: DUKE OF DANGER *coming September 2015!*

REQUEST YOUR FREE BOOKS!

HARLEQUIN®

ℍISTORICAL

Where love is timeless

2 FREE NOVELS PLUS 2 **FREE GIFTS!**

YES! Please send me 2 FREE Harlequin® Historical novels and my 2 FREE gifts (gifts are worth about $10). After receiving them, if I don't wish to receive any more books, I can return the shipping statement marked "cancel." If I don't cancel, I will receive 6 brand-new novels every month and be billed just $5.69 per book in the U.S. or $5.99 per book in Canada. That's a savings of at least 12% off the cover price! It's quite a bargain! Shipping and handling is just 50¢ per book in the U.S. and 75¢ per book in Canada.* I understand that accepting the 2 free books and gifts places me under no obligation to buy anything. I can always return a shipment and cancel at any time. Even if I never buy another book, the two free books and gifts are mine to keep forever.

246/349 HDN GH2Z

Name	(PLEASE PRINT)
Address	Apt. #
City	State/Prov.	Zip/Postal Code

Signature (if under 18, a parent or guardian must sign)

Mail to the **Reader Service:**
IN U.S.A.: P.O. Box 1867, Buffalo, NY 14240-1867
IN CANADA: P.O. Box 609, Fort Erie, Ontario L2A 5X3

**Want to try two free books from another line?
Call 1-800-873-8635 or visit www.ReaderService.com.**

* Terms and prices subject to change without notice. Prices do not include applicable taxes. Sales tax applicable in N.Y. Canadian residents will be charged applicable taxes. Offer not valid in Quebec. This offer is limited to one order per household. Not valid for current subscribers to Harlequin Historical books. All orders subject to credit approval. Credit or debit balances in a customer's account(s) may be offset by any other outstanding balance owed by or to the customer. Please allow 4 to 6 weeks for delivery. Offer available while quantities last.

Your Privacy—The Reader Service is committed to protecting your privacy. Our Privacy Policy is available online at www.ReaderService.com or upon request from the Reader Service.

We make a portion of our mailing list available to reputable third parties that offer products we believe may interest you. If you prefer that we not exchange your name with third parties, or if you wish to clarify or modify your communication preferences, please visit us at www.ReaderService.com/consumerchoice or write to us at Reader Service Preference Service, P.O. Box 9062, Buffalo, NY 14240-9062. Include your complete name and address.

HH15

He turned towards her, using the pillar as a barrier so that they were cut off from the hearing of those around them, but she knew that it would not be many seconds before the world around them impinged again.

"You would be bored to death with Freddy Lovelace in a week."

"Could we meet privately, then?" She made herself say the words, hating the desperation so obvious within them.

"Pardon?"

"I need to know what it would be like to touch a man who might make my heart beat faster before I settle for one who does not. Your reputation heralds a great proficiency in such matters, and I thought perhaps you might…"

"Hell, Adelaide."

The horror of everything spiraled in her head. She had asked for something so dreadful that even the most dissolute lover in all of London town could not accommodate her.

"I…can't."

His voice was strangled and rough, the words like darts as she turned on her heels, hoping he did not see the tears that were threatening to fall as she walked briskly from his side.

Don't miss
MARRIAGE MADE IN SHAME by Sophia James,
available September 2015 wherever
Harlequin® Historical books and ebooks are sold.

www.Harlequin.com